X 7/99

CYBER BRIDE

CYBER BRIDE

•

Annette Couch-Jareb

AVALON BOOKS
NEW YORK

PRINTED IN THE UNITED STATES OF AMERICA
ON ACID-FREE PAPER
BY HADDON CRAFTSMEN, BLOOMSBURG, PENNSYLVANIA

For Ivo, the better-than-fiction hero.

Chapter One

. . . Cyber Scribe: I feel like we've shared so much of ourselves, yet I know so little about you. What do you do for a living?
DaVinci: You can't tell from my "name?"
Cyber Scribe: You don't have to tell if you don't want to. That's the joy of cyber space—anonymity.
DaVinci: No big secret. I'm a painter.
Cyber Scribe: Of houses?
DaVinci: No. I'm painting right now.
Cyber Scribe: While we're talking? What are you painting?

Kate held up the leg bone to get a closer look at the pits and blemishes, then turned back to her keyboard.

DaVinci: A nude.
Cyber Scribe: Lucky dog. I think I took up the wrong profession.
DaVinci: It's not as glamorous as it sounds.

She thought how truly unglamorous her work must seem to someone else. She sat alone all day with only the company of Fritz, her cat. Her only human contact—aside from her cyborg compadres on the Internet and her neighbors in the high-rise where she lived—was her agent. Kate preferred it that way. People were complicated. Her agent filtered out the rest of the world for her. She was in demand as a scientific illustrator, so

1

she never needed to pound the pavement for work. Now that she had made a name for herself in the field, work came to her via her agent. No coworkers meant no uncomfortable entanglements.

There was a long pause before she received a response from "Cyber Scribe."

> *Cyber Scribe: You must be quite skilled to be able to work and type at the same time. I, however, cannot. I'll have to leave off. Talk to you later.*
> *DaVinci: Later, friend.*

Kate switched off her computer and placed the leg bone back in the case with the rest of the remains. As her own boss, she could take a break from work to do her laundry. Besides, she had already more than met her deadline. She snapped the lid closed on the metal case of bones with which she had been entrusted for this assignment, then she covered her sketches with a piece of tissue paper.

Kate enjoyed her work and she never really felt as though she was working alone. With the computer on all day and the regulars on her chat group, she felt as if she had an office that she went to and a regular group of coworkers. Over the course of a year, she had become well acquainted with the regulars and she considered "Cyber Scribe" to be her best friend. Who needed real-life buddies when such friends were to be had over the 'Net?

The elevator doors closed. Kate balanced a laundry basket of clean clothes on her hip, then pressed number 16 and waited for the familiar stomach-tickling lift. Stops were as much fun and Kate smiled when one floor up, at the lobby, the elevator stopped again. Vanilla Lady was waiting at the door, leaning on her walker. Kate stepped to the side. The old lady smelled like vanilla and Kate decided when she was old that she would like to smell like vanilla, too. She would remember to take the extract out of the kitchen cupboard when she got home and put it on the bathroom sink.

Hippie Guy from the fifteenth floor came through the main

door into the lobby. He was wet from the rain. A seemingly sweet fellow, he was someone with whom she might have been able to strike up a friendship. However, he had the misfortune of working with animals, so he usually came in smelling like a dog. She couldn't see herself inviting him up for coffee if he was going to freak out her cat with his doggy smell. Today he smelled like a wet dog. She only hoped that Vanilla Lady could counteract him. Kate quickly pushed the OPEN button to hold the elevator for him.

She immediately regretted her thoughtfulness. Outside, through the lobby door, Suit Man was just coming in out of the rain. He was always in a hurry. He was either hurrying onto the elevator or hurrying off. The one time she had bumped into him in the laundry room, he was hurrying to do his laundry, mixing his whites with his darks just to have done with the job. Lucky for him his suits were dry-cleaned. Today he saw that the elevator was waiting, so he hurried his step to get there before the doors closed. He wore his usual serious expression. Because of Vanilla Lady's walker, Hippie Guy was slow in boarding. Suit Man was halfway across the lobby. Kate could not very well hold the door for Hippie Guy, but let it slam in the face of Suit Man. Instead, she smiled sweetly as he curtly nodded his thanks to her. As a general rule, no one spoke on the elevator.

Kate moved closer to the control panel, then greeted Hippie Guy. "Fifteenth floor?"

The man with the red frizzled hair blinked hard at her. "Fifth, actually, but how'd you know I live on the fifteenth?"

"I've seen you get on and off the elevator before. Fifth floor it is, then." And without further chitchat, she pressed button number 5.

Because Suit Man was on the other side of Vanilla Lady, he also spoke up. "Twentieth floor for me."

Kate pressed the button, then turned to stare at the closed doors in front of her. Of course he would live on the top floor. Those on the top floor were the most sought-after apartments. Kate wondered how many "Vanilla Ladies" he had trampled to get it.

"Wretched weather today." Vanilla Lady broke tradition by speaking.

"You weren't planning on going out in it, were you?" Kate decided if everyone else was breaking the rules, she could also.

Vanilla Lady smiled sweetly. "It's grocery day—eggs, bread, milk—but that can wait until tomorrow. I got to the door and turned right back around. I don't want to risk breaking the other hip."

Kate smiled, adjusted the basket of laundry on her hip, then put her other hand on her stomach as the elevator came to a stop. She wasn't aware of the attention her action elicited from Suit Man. He watched as she smiled at the stomach-tickling stop.

Hippie Guy moved toward the open elevator doors, then wafted off, and the doors closed, leaving him and his wet aroma on the fifth floor. There was an almost audible sigh of relief from those remaining.

There was silence on the elevator again until they reached the twelfth floor—home of Vanilla Lady.

"Pardon me." Suit Man stepped off of the elevator before her to make way for her walker. He held the doors open with his hand even though Kate held the OPEN button, and then he stepped back inside. They both watched Vanilla Lady fumbling for the key secreted in the pouch that dangled from her walker.

The doors closed on the elevator and they waited through that awkward silence before the elevator began its ascent. "That's the only thing that scares me about getting old," Suit Man broke elevator silence, then turned to face Kate. "To be old and alone. Having an infirmity on top of it must be awful."

Kate noticed his hair was graying at the temples. "So, you don't live alone?" Judging from his laundry habits she had been almost certain that he was single.

Suit Man smiled. "Meaning I'm already halfway there?" He read her thoughts and ran a hand roughly through his graying hair.

"Oh, no!" she hurriedly amended. "I didn't mean to imply

that you were old. You're very distinguished-looking.'' She cringed at her own choice of words. "I didn't mean that either. You're very handsome.'' Again she cringed and put her fingertips to her lips. "Let me just stop while I still have a scrap of dignity left.''

Now Suit Man was grinning. Kate didn't think she had ever seen him so much as crack a smile. He was indeed very handsome when he smiled.

"Thank you, I think.''

Kate's cheeks burned and she turned to stare at the closed doors again, praying they would open immediately. She'd get off on any floor.

"You're Kate.''

Kate turned back around to stare at him drop-jawed. "Yes.'' She wasn't quite sure why she said it, probably because he had the upper hand in the introductions, but she returned, "And you're Suit Man.''

"Suit Man?'' He laughed and she resented it.

She had left herself open to conversation with this stranger.

"Well, yes. You know how no one ever introduces themselves on the elevator. So I make up names for them. You're Suit Man. The lady we just dropped off is Vanilla Lady and before that, we left Hippie Guy on the fifth floor.''

"Fitting descriptions, all of them, and none of them ungenerous.'' Then taking Kate by surprise, he extended his hand. "Allow me to introduce myself.'' Kate was disconcerted, but adjusted her load and met his grip with her free hand. "Edward. Virgil Edward Tucker, a.k.a. Suit Man'' and for the first time since Kate could remember, Suit Man did not seem to be in a rush.

"Nice to meet you, Virgil. As you already seem to know, I'm Kate. Kate Delaney.''

The familiar ping sounded as the elevator reached the sixteenth floor. "I'll be bumping into you later, Suit Man.'' And she backed off.

The doors closed between them before he had a chance to tell her that *no one* called him by his first name.

Back in her apartment Kate put the basket of laundry down in the middle of the living room floor and did an about-face.

She was forever forgetting her dryer sheets in the laundry room and if she didn't retrieve them immediately, they'd be gone when she went back down for the second load of clothes.

Back down on the elevator she went. The elevator stopped on the fourteenth floor to admit two other residents of the high-rise apartment. Gypsy Girl and her boyfriend, Significant Other, S.O. for short, boarded. They were still in the kissy-huggy stage of their relationship and they held hands on the ride down to the lobby, whispering to each other as they descended.

Kate recalled a time when she had thought herself to be in love. They had worked together for the same magazine, but a company rule about nepotism kept them from revealing their office romance. Secretly, on the elevator up to their shared office, they would hold hands and whisper loverly things to each other—just like Gypsy Girl and S.O.—until the doors would open to admit one or another of their coworkers. Kate had thought it was all great fun—this wonderful secret romance—until it had stopped being fun.

The elevator doors opened at the lobby and Gypsy Girl and S.O. stepped off. The doors were just about to close again when Kate saw past the couple to the outside lobby doors. Suit Man was leaving again and in the pouring rain. She watched as he rushed off down the street and wondered if, like her, he had just forgotten something, maybe in his car or back at his office. The doors closed and he was cut off from her view.

Downstairs in the laundry room, Kate walked in just in time to catch the washing machine as it did a dance in the floor. Quickly, she opened the lid to shift her load. Good thing she had come back for the dryer sheets, she thought, then decided to stick around until the end of the wash cycle. No sense coming back in fifteen minutes only to find that the washer had automatically shut off because of an unbalanced load. Kate made herself comfortable on top of the washer and read the box of dryer sheets from cover to cover, removed her laundry when the cycle finished and threw it into a dryer, then left to hop on the elevator again.

Again, the elevator stopped at the lobby as it almost always did. For the second time that day, Kate held the OPEN button to admit Suit Man, who was just returning. He held a slightly damp bag of groceries in his arms.

"Thanks, Kate."

Kate smiled at him, but he was all seriousness again. He was just reaching for the control panel when Kate intercepted.

"Allow me. I'm in training for this profession, you know." She pressed the button for the twentieth floor.

Virgil Edward Tucker had transformed back into Suit Man and gave her only a curt nod, so with no opening for continued conversation, Kate turned back to face the doors. It seemed to take forever before the elevator finally pinged at the sixteenth floor.

"Nice chatting with you, Virgil," she sarcastically flung over her shoulder as she stepped off. It seemed her first impression of him had been correct. He was always in a hurry. He was probably a shut-in, she imagined, then turned to watch the lights above the elevator as they blinked past 17, 18, 19, then 20. The light stopped, then almost immediately began a descent. Nineteen, 18 . . . 16 . . . finally coming to stop on the twelfth floor.

"What are you up to, Suit Man?" Kate said to no one, wondering why he had not just told her he was going to the twelfth floor. The elevator remained fixed on that floor for nearly half a minute, then it began a climb up again. It stopped on the twentieth floor, this time long enough for someone to actually disembark.

Hastily, Kate pressed the elevator button. She knew it was nosy, but not so much so that she would lose sleep over it. She had an idea she knew what had happened, and that sort of thing just didn't happen in the big city. Suit Man must be some sort of throwback. The elevator arrived and Kate jumped on. She pressed the button for the twelfth floor several times as if that would make the elevator move faster. At the usual stomach-tickling speed, it descended then stopped. The doors opened and Kate poked her head around the door, only long enough to confirm her suspicions. Suit Man had placed the bag of groceries he had been carrying in front of Vanilla

Lady's door. She was just taking them in, her back to the elevator.

Hastily, Kate ducked back inside and pressed several buttons at once.

"Hey, you there," Vanilla Lady called.

Kate hastily pressed the CLOSE button. Vanilla Lady was moving toward the elevator, but Kate stepped back into the corner to go unseen. The doors closed and the elevator began a descent.

Suit Man might be a weird bird, but he was a *sweet* weird bird.

When Kate remembered herself, she pressed the button to her own floor, then rode the elevator up one more time.

DaVinci: Hey, Cyber Scribe! Are you out there?

There was no response, so Kate typed the code that would make his computer ping if he had it on to indicate that he was receiving a personal call.

Cyber Scribe: Hello there, DaVinci. Long time no hear.

DaVinci: Yeah. Listen. I just had the strangest introduction. Wanna hear a personal story of love and intrigue?

Cyber Scribe: You bet!

DaVinci: I just met this fellow on the elevator—a weird bird—always very serious, in a rush all the time. I finally got an introduction today and then the strangest thing happened. There's an old lady who lives in our apartment building. This fellow goes out in the pouring rain and buys her a bag of groceries. Can you believe it?

Cyber Scribe: Sounds like a kook to me. You mean he told you he went out and did this wonderful act?

DaVinci: No! And don't try to burst my bubble. It was very sweet. This guy rides up on the elevator with me. I forget my dryer sheets in the laundry room, so when I go down I see this guy going out again into the pouring rain. When I come back up, he's on the elevator again with a bag of groceries in his arm. He rides the elevator up like he's going home only he doesn't get off. I saw the lights over the elevator blink and he rides back down to the old lady's floor.

Cyber Scribe: *And you surmise all this from the lights on the elevator?*

DaVinci: *No. Supersleuth that I am, I ride down to the old lady's floor and sure enough, there's the bag of wet groceries and the old lady just taking them in. She didn't see me, though.*

Cyber Scribe: *Pretty sneaky.*

DaVinci: *Yeah, so what do you think?*

Cyber Scribe: *I think you've got too much time on your hands.*

DaVinci: *Be serious. Do you think I should strike up a friendship with this fellow? He's a little bit older than me.*

Cyber Scribe: *Why not? Maybe he'll leave a bag of groceries on your doorstep.*

Kate laughed, then signed off.

Virgil Edward Tucker, Tucker to all of his poker friends, pushed his oak desk chair away from his computer keyboard. A scowl marred his brow. He hated being found out and he wished he had not bothered about getting the old lady her "eggs, bread, and milk." Kate was sweet, but like the old lady—what did Kate call her? Vanilla Lady? He smiled. Like Vanilla Lady, Kate was a project. It wasn't right that she should stay so secluded from the world. She had only moved into his apartment building a little under a year ago, but she had yet to make friends with any of her neighbors and he believed she worked out of her home. That did not give anyone a lot of opportunity to meet people. Tucker had taken it upon himself to befriend her. Also, like all of his other projects, he told himself his motives where Kate was concerned were completely unselfish. They had an almost intimate relationship over the Internet, but she was definitely lacking in the real-life realm of friends. He intended to rectify that.

*   *   *

Kate dug through the handbags on the floor of her closet, grabbed up her small sequined clutch, threw in a pair of black onyx earrings and the matching necklace from the jewelry box nestled on the floor beside her mattress, then dashed out the door. She was going to be late again and David, her agent, would be in a snit all evening. These openings were enough of a drag without putting her escort into a foul mood as well. Her tardiness had everything to do with her lack of enthusiasm over the evening ahead.

David always only called her at the last minute, although he had known about and been planning this opening for the past six months. He expected her to show up in her finest, hobnob with everyone he had wrangled into coming to see her work, then he would ditch her to saddle up beside some tall blond for the rest of the evening. She would be left trying to understand the free-associative thought flow of some elderly woman in a white turban or some young art student dressed in black. David wasn't even paying her the courtesy of picking her up. She'd have to catch a cab to her own opening.

She was donning her left shoe when the elevator doors opened in front of her.

"Good evening, Kate Delaney."

Kate looked up to see Suit Man standing in front of her and as if they were off on an evening together, he was every bit her equal as far as attire. He wore a double-breasted suit and conservative black shoes. The only daring part of his attire was a green-and-purple paisley tie.

"Hi!" was all she could gurgle out. She had been planning for a week what she would say when they bumped into each other again. In her scenario she was already on the elevator and he just stepping on from the lobby. She would have the upper hand because she was privy to his good deed to Vanilla Lady. She had been carrying around a "buy one, get one free" coffee coupon in her handbag—her everyday handbag—and she would invite him to join her around the corner at the coffee shop. In her imaginings, she wouldn't lose her nerve and she certainly wouldn't find herself tongue-tied.

"Hi," she repeated herself, then winced.

"It's Suit Man," he reintroduced himself, pointing his thumb at his own chest.

Kate smiled and nodded. "I know." Then nodding toward his chest, she added, "That's a pretty dapper suit you're wearing tonight, Virgil."

"You too, if I may add." And he took in all of her, starting at her flat black shoes and moving up her fitted black dress which rose to her neck in a conservative collar, yet left her arms and shoulders bare. "Saturday night. Big date?"

Kate's eyebrows drew together as she considered her answer. It seemed somehow immodest to tell him she was going to her own opening.

"More of an obligation."

"Oh, sorry." And he genuinely seemed sorry.

"No. Don't be." She didn't want him to think she was going on a mercy date. "I mean, it's work related." They grew silent as the elevator descended, then Kate tacked on, "And you? Big date?"

"Wallflower."

"Huh?" While she waited for an explanation she dug in her purse for the earrings she had tossed in in her hurry out the door.

He smiled, then went on to explain. "Also business related, so I'm not going to bore and neglect a date."

Kate added that to her memory. Suit Man was conscientious as well. "Well, I find it doubtful you turn out to be much of a wallflower wherever you are going." Kate slipped on the second earring, then found the matching necklace in her handbag. She held the clasp behind her neck and fumbled with the catch for a moment.

"Here. Allow me." And by unspoken consent, Kate turned her back to him and lifted her wavy, shoulder-length hair to better enable him to fasten the clasp. It was an oddly personal thing to allow a near-complete stranger to do, but since seeing his kind act to Vanilla Lady, Kate felt she knew him, or at least wouldn't mind getting to know him better.

"Very pretty."

"Thank you. It was a gift from Harry." And she knew he wasn't referring to only her necklace, but she left the compliment to go unthanked. She preferred to believe he was just admiring the family heirloom her grandfather had given her.

The elevator doors opened onto the lobby just as Edward was dropping her hair to cover her shoulders again. Kate looked up in time to see Hippie Guy watching them in the lobby and she blushed. There was nothing wrong with their actions, yet she felt she had done something forward in allowing any of their neighbors to see them getting off the elevator together.

Kate impatiently looked at the delicate gold watch on her wrist, gave Hippie Guy a cursory nod, then stepped out into the alcove between the two sets of double glass doors that led outside. It was raining outside and Kate had not thought to bring an umbrella. She felt herself prepared in that she remembered to grab her wallet.

Suit Man saw her action and stopped in the alcove with her. "I can wait with you until your date arrives."

"Oh, it's not my date. I called a cab twenty minutes ago, knowing that it would be late, and true to form it's not here. David will be a bear if I'm much later than I already am."

"A cab? Your date isn't picking you up? Oh, that's right. You said it was business related." He unbuttoned the bottom button of his jacket then pushed it up on the side to reach into his trousers pocket. "I'm parked just down the block. I'd be happy to give you a lift."

Kate thrilled at the prospect. Could it possibly be any easier to strike up an acquaintance? And how silly the whole idea now seemed of saving her coffee coupon.

"Oh, thank you! I wouldn't trouble you ordinarily, but you'd really be saving my neck. You see, I was supposed to be at the Museum entrance with my agent this evening, greeting people as they came."

He nodded. "The Dabney Museum," he stated her destination as if he knew.

"Why, yes," Kate held the handrail and fell into quickened step beside him. "But, could it be possible . . ." She knew from his smile that it was possible.

"I have a confession to make." He smiled at her. "That's

where I'm headed." Then he explained, "I saw the announcement in the art section of the newspaper last Sunday."

"You said on business. Surely an opening isn't business?"

Suit Man smiled mischievously. "Actually I have ulterior motives. I only recently learned that you are Kate Delaney— the artist. I've been trying to commission some work, but can't seem to get around your agent. I had hoped that tonight I could explain what I'm looking for and, per your acceptance, deal with you personally."

Warning bells went off in Kate's head and she stopped on the sidewalk beside the conservative black car which Suit Man was indicating to be his own. He looked up when she didn't move to climb in, but instead stood in drizzling rain.

"Oh, Kate. I'm sorry. You must think I'm some sort of stalker. I didn't mean—" But she cut him off.

"No, Virgil, not at all. I'm very flattered." But that was precisely how she had felt for a split-second due to no fault of his. For an instant she had reverted to that time in her life when she had had to watch over her shoulder for just such a stalker. It was her office romance all over again.

When she had learned that her coworker/fiancé had a secret romance with another coworker, Kate had tried to end it. When she stopped returning his calls, the harassing phone calls had begun and later on, he would lurk outside her apartment at night. If she went out on a date, he would meet her and her date at her door when they came home, just to make certain the evening ended with a handshake. Finally, it had become such a horrible situation, Kate had had to get a restraining order and finally left her job with the magazine. In the case of Suit Man, which, she wondered, had come first? His desire to have a painting commissioned or his finding out that the Dabney Museum was going to show her work? Was he just using the commission as a ploy? Was it just coincidence that he had been on the elevator this evening, or had he been lurking in the elevator waiting for her to board? She looked up at his eyes which were still surveying her. He had taken his hand away from the door latch. He was visibly distressed that she might believe his motives were anything but proper. She recognized his sincerity almost immediately and felt guilty and more than a little paranoid.

"No, Virgil. Sorry. I'm just a little gun-shy. I want to hear more about this commission."

They talked in his car on the way to the opening.

"So, your agent believed I wanted to hang your artwork in a hotel lobby or something, but I assure you, it's nothing of the sort. I've heard your name and seen your work before in some of the most respected science journals. As my publishing house begins publication of a new science journal we want to start with a bang. Your artwork is recognizable in the field. I don't believe I'm being overly generous when I say your art-work adds credence to the professionalism of the journal."

"And my agent, David, is being hard-nosed about my 'backsliding,' as he calls it, into the world of graphic arts?" Kate knew her agent had high expectations for her work that did not include functionality. He was every bit the snob where art was concerned. Kate had been the only artist he had ever taken on who was not interested in a career in the fine arts. She was happy illustrating medical textbooks and science jour-nals, but he insisted that she would never make a name for herself in graphic arts and thus, she would never command the magnificent salaries from which he hoped to earn his commission.

"I can't really fault him," Suit Man defended her agent. "Like I said, I've seen your work before and it's everything an art connoisseur could want in a painting. You have an amazing talent for creating, as you call it, a 'functional' piece of work, which is so deeply layered as to make it a real piece of art."

"Well, I can answer for my agent. I'd be happy to work with you on your new project—and not just because you've flattered my work into the realm of the unbelievable." Suit Man laughed as he maneuvered his car into a parallel parking space just a few blocks from the Dabney Museum. "I rather feel like I'm being pushed into a profession that I don't fancy. I'm not of that ethereal world of fine arts. I'm an illustrator and I can't think of any greater goal to attain than that my work be useful to someone. If I can convey a new medical procedure in drawing where words and explanations fail, then I've accomplished something that I can be proud of. I don't think Harry would be too awfully proud of me if my paintings were just hanging on a museum wall someplace for people to study and to ponder the different dimensions. If there's anything to my work other than an illustration, it's because I was bored with the project and wanted to throw in a couple of visual puns.''

Suit Man was scowling, so Kate brought it to his attention.

''You know, Suit Man, you have a very serious demeanor. It makes you somewhat unapproachable.'' He turned in his seat to face her, so she continued with a cheery smile. ''I'm glad I was able to catch a ride with you tonight. I think this evening might even be bearable now.''

In fact, her evening and her acquaintance with Virgil were both turning out to be nothing like she had anticipated. Before she could unbuckle her seat belt he was holding her door for her. Not only was she not attending the opening alone, but Suit Man offered her his arm as they ascended the ten steps into the brownstone that had been converted into a glamorous and trendy museum. She released his arm at the top of the stairs, then entered as he held the door for her. Almost before she had a chance to thank him, however, she was swooped upon by David, her agent.

''Katherine, love.'' He kissed her on her cheek, but whispered in a harsh tone, ''You're late, darling. In the future, please save being fashionably late for the truly famous artists.'' Then he said in a louder voice, ''There's someone here just dying to meet you,'' and he pulled her away from her escort.

Kate carefully detached herself from his grip on her upper arm, then whispered back to him, ''David, in the future, please reserve your rudeness for the truly deserving,'' and before they had reached the person on the other side of the gallery to whom he had intended to introduce her, she did an about-face and returned to Virgil's side.

David was on her heels and gave Kate's ''date'' the once-over. ''But of course. Please introduce me to your father, Katherine.''

Kate gave her agent a glaring look that might have shriveled a less egocentric person, but she smiled up at Virgil. He was tall, even by David's standards, and David stood at least an inch over six feet. Also, as she had told him in the elevator when they were introduced, he really was quite handsome. His hair was dark with just a touch of gray at the temples. In his dark suit, he posed an awesome picture and when they had entered the museum, Kate knew the appreciative looks they had received—at least those from the women in the room— were for his benefit. Tonight, his hair was combed back away from his forehead and still had the appearance of being damp from his shower. She had noticed in the car the scent of soap and a masculine aftershave and in the museum, in the flatter- ing light, he did not look as old as she had at first imagined him to be.

"David Tipton, I'd like to introduce you to—" But Virgil cut her off.

"V. Edward Tucker. Everyone just calls me Edward." Then as an aside to Kate, he said, "No one ever calls me by my first name and I'll have to swear you to secrecy over that." He turned his attention back to the art agent. "You and I spoke over the phone, and Kate and I are no relation."

Kate looked up at Edward with a smile, but didn't comment on his abbreviated name. She would savor the secret she shared with him.

David took his extended hand, but only hesitantly. "Ah, yes, the magazine."

"Actually," Kate corrected, "it is a science journal, and Mr. Tucker"—she looked to him for confirmation that she was correct in not using his first name—"has commissioned me to do some work for the first issue."

"Well, we'll discuss that later." And for the second time, David took Kate's upper arm, only this time a bit more pain- fully. "I'm glad to see you've developed an appreciation for Katherine's work as something more than illustrative. I have high hopes for Katherine's future as an artist. I'm sure you can appreciate and respect the politics involved in making the sort of career transition she is making."

Kate pried his hand from her arm, this time not bothering

to be discreet about it. "Mr. Tucker has been very complimentary. I think he understands where I'm coming from in my work." Then she said more to Edward, "If you don't mind, I'd love to do the circuit with you." And without waiting for him to offer, she linked her arm under his. Edward nodded and she turned back to David. "Now, who was it you wanted me to meet?"

David's expression held daggers for Kate, but that was something that only someone who knew him well would be able to see. She could tell they would have a huge argument later about the direction her work was taking. David tended to be very territorial about his clients' work, but Kate was prepared to find herself another agent if he wasn't working for her instead of the other way around.

David chose to completely ignore Edward and directed his short, staccato directions to Kate. "This fellow you're about to meet is Dr. John Post. He's on the board of some *very* serious endowments." David whispered into her ear, not attempting to take her free arm, but simply leaning in, "Please don't mention the word 'illustration.' " As quickly, he brightened, turning on his fake charm. "John. Delighted you could make it." He did a "ta-da" with his hands toward Kate. "Here she is. The woman I've been telling you about."

Kate took his proffered hand, then immediately introduced her escort.

The next two hours proceeded in roughly the same manner, with Kate being introduced to the influential elite of the art world while Edward unreservedly pretended to be her date. He left her side just once when she was engaged by another artist to discuss the intricacies of light and shadow in her work, but he returned after a brief visit to the open bar and handed her a glass of white wine.

It was the first opportunity Kate had had to glance at the delicate watch on her wrist and she gasped.

"Oh, Edward, I had no idea I had kept you so late."

But he was already shaking his head and swallowed the wine he had just taken in before speaking. "Not at all. It has all been extremely enlightening."

Kate leaned in to whisper in his ear, "Pretentious and self-absorbed.'' Then as she pulled away from him, she said, ''Forgive me?''

Edward smiled down at her, shaking his head. ''You loved it. Are you sure you don't enjoy the idea of your work hanging on a museum wall? Perhaps I've cornered you into something you don't really want. Maybe your agent *does* know what is best for your career.''

Out of the corner of her eye, Kate saw David homing in on her and she decided it was a good time to make an exit. David could explain her abbreviated appearance at her own opening as some sort of artistic foible. Quickly, she looped her arm back in Edward's.

''Do you mind if we make a hasty getaway?''

Reading her thoughts as he too saw that she was about to be descended upon, he maneuvered her behind a pillar, then toward the exit. Outside, she felt the strain of introductions and limelight melt from her shoulders. She stretched her back with her free hand on her spine, then released Edward from her grip. It had stopped raining.

She was silent for the entire two-block walk back to Edward's car. It wasn't until she was seated on the passenger side and he behind the wheel that she finally broke the silence.

''You know, you're right. I do enjoy the spotlight—for about an hour. Who wouldn't be flattered by all that attention and praise, but . . .'' And she trailed off as she fumbled for the right words. ''There has to be a solid center to one's work. It's like Harry says: if your pride comes for a fleeting few minutes of adulation, then what is there to comfort you the other twenty-three hours and fifty-seven minutes of the day?'' She thought about her grandfather's words for a second, then turned to stare out of the passenger-side window at the lamplit street outside and the shiny reflection it made on the wet sidewalk. ''No. It's the illustrating that gives me that comfort.'' She turned back to face Edward who had been intently watching the side of her face. ''All that''—she pointed toward the museum—''that's all meringue. You think the pie looks so delicious, but all that froufrou just sort of melts in your mouth without a lot of taste.''

Edward was smiling at her and Kate was momentarily mesmerized as she studied the divot under his bottom lip. She was still caught up in the unreality of the whole evening. It would take her several more hours at home alone before she finally came back to earth, but Edward's presence only made it seem more like a dream. After all, she had not known him just a few short days ago and now, they had, for all intents and purposes, just shared a date.

It was dreamlike the way he had been at her side all evening, like a magic amulet to protect her from her agent. Even while he had remained silent while she spoke with art enthusiasts about her work, his presence had always been there. He had listened to all that was said and watched her every movement and expression. He was still doing it in the car. She felt a magnetic pull from him and almost felt as if their faces were drawing closer together. It was as if their lips were on a collision course. She felt her eyelids flutter heavily, then . . .

"I hate meringue, too."

Her eyes snapped open and she pulled back the inch she had allowed herself to drift toward him.

He was still smiling at her, but all too soon he turned away from her and turned the key in the ignition. Kate slumped back against the seat. Just when she thought she could ride on the surrealistic cloud for the rest of the evening, she had found herself snapped back to her center.

It was Suit Man seated beside her again. He was still handsome, in a neighborly sort of way, but she would very soon be commissioned by him. Best, she thought, to keep things on a very professional level. She knew, all too well, the pitfalls of becoming involved with someone with whom one worked.

Chapter Two

Virgil Edward Tucker flipped the ON switch on the back of his computer after unbuttoning his coat, but before loosening the purple-and-green paisley necktie. It automatically logged on with two clicks of the mouse and he was on-line with his Internet cronies almost before he had lost the scent of her perfume.

He suspected her habits were similar. She always seemed to be on-line, and he imagined her coming in from their date, throwing down her purse, then immediately switching on her computer. He drummed his fingers impatiently for five minutes with no sign of her on the screen. It was possible, since she lived on the sixteenth floor and he on the twentieth, that she had managed to log on before he had made it home and switched on his computer, in which case he could have missed the computer announcement that *"DaVinci has entered the room."* On the off chance that she was merely lurking, reading the open messages that the other people on the chat group wrote, Edward performed a search to see which people were on-line. "Damsel, Life Guard, Flea, Bronte . . ." He stood, leaning over the keyboard as he read the list aloud and unbuttoning his shirt, then he pulled the desk chair around behind him without looking and sat back.

Was it ethical, he wondered, to continue chatting with Kate—DaVinci—and not reveal who he was? She had flinched this evening when he had surprised her by admitting he was going to her opening. She really had felt trespassed upon at first even though she had said she had not. How might she feel if he revealed himself as her computer pal, Cyber

Scribe? It had been an innocent enough meeting. They had both been involved in a chat group related to the publishing industry. Their first on-line debates had been passionate, but they were respectful of each other's opinions. Over the course of several months, they had come to "know" each other extremely well although they had no physical notion of who the other was.

It might have remained so, too, if Kate had taken the precautions she should have to protect her anonymity. Probably a novice to the whole world of cyberspace, she had not hidden her identity behind a password. As it was, Cyber Scribe had only to "finger" her pseudonym, DaVinci, to learn her real name. The name had sounded familiar, so he had proceeded to look her up in the phone book. There was no listing, but certain he had heard the name before, he buzzed his secretary and asked him to check the tenant files for Katherine Delaney. Sure enough, he had a tenant in his high-rise apartment building by the same name. Certain there must be more than one Katherine Delaney in the big city, he had asked her what her occupation was to confirm his suspicions. The tenant in his building had put on her application for tenancy, "scientific illustrator." DaVinci described herself as a painter. It had to be one and the same person. The odds of anyone in the chat group living in the same town, much less in the same building, were astronomical, yet there was no other explanation.

Suddenly, he saw what he had been waiting for. "*DaVinci has entered the room*" appeared on the computer screen. He waited, not wanting to be the first to strike up a conversation. He still had not hashed out the whole ethical thing.

DaVinci: Hey, Cyber Scribe. I see you're in the room, but are you at your computer?

Edward pulled his seat closer to the keyboard, then took a deep breath. He recognized his own attraction to Kate. He did not want to make a fool of himself by pursuing her if she was repulsed by him. He was supposed to be concerned about her reclusiveness. He didn't want to scare her back into hiding from whatever she was avoiding.

Cyber Scribe: Good evening.
DaVinci: Have I missed any excitement this evening?
Cyber Scribe: I've only just come on-line myself.
DaVinci: Hurrah for us! We have a life!
Cyber Scribe: Big date?
DaVinci: You're the second person this evening to ask me that. Actually, I took my own advice and managed to strike up an acquaintance with the "kook," as you called him.
Cyber Scribe: Did you get free groceries out of it?
DaVinci: Not so much as a candy bar.
Cyber Scribe: Better luck next time.

Edward signed off. He felt morally compromised and more than a little bit ashamed of his behavior. He had no right to eavesdrop on her conversation with Cyber Scribe—even if he was the confidant. At the same time, however, the temptation was incredibly strong to draw Kate out on one minor point. When they had first entered the museum, he had felt a strange abandonment when Kate's agent, David Tipton, had taken her arm to escort her toward an introduction, but it had not taken a psychic to figure out that they were at odds with each other and that he posed no competition. There was, however, the mention of another man, Harry, who seemed to play a domi- nant role in her life. Who was this Harry whom she had men- tioned on no less than two occassions during the evening? What sort of relationship did they share that she could speak so highly of him, yet he never come to visit her? To the best of his knowledge, he had never known her to have long-term visitors to her apartment. That was the sort of thing that one generally noticed living in the same building. Perhaps Kate did have a life outside of her apartment of which he simply was not aware. How could he draw Kate out about Harry without letting on that Cyber Scribe and Virgil Edward Tucker were one and the same person?

Edward shook his head and pushed his chair away from the computer. He'd have to wrestle with the moral implications before he spoke again to DaVinci. Then he wondered if he was reading more into his chances with Kate than actually existed.

For a moment before they had begun the car ride home he had thought she was going to kiss him, but that certainly could not have been the case. It must, he convinced himself, have been his own imagination. Kate was tired after the long evening and felt relaxed enough with him to let down some of her usual defenses. He could find something to be flattered about in that alone and probably should not scratch any deeper, he decided.

He sat back and allowed his memory to rekindle their parting just a few short minutes ago. They had reached the apartment building, he had held her door for her again, but she had made no attempt to take his arm as she had throughout the evening. It had been a long time since anyone had done that. Even his wife, when she had been alive, had rarely held his hand. She had not been a demonstrative woman. Edward shook his head. He still felt guilty about comparing any woman to his deceased wife.

Probably a sign of his healing, he quickly recognized, and dismissed his guilt and reverted to his thoughts about Kate. He had the impression that Kate probably was demonstrative toward those for whom she cared. Not that she had left him on the elevator that evening with anything more than a businesslike handshake.

As they had stepped onto the elevator he had wrestled with the dilemma: should he see her to her door, or simply continue up on the elevator? She had answered the question for him. Before the elevator pinged at the sixteenth floor, she had extended her hand to him.

"I'm very grateful to you for all you've done tonight, Edward." She looked down at the floor and smiled. "That's so funny to say."

"Yeah, about that. No one calls me by my first name. I usually guard it with my life. I have several friends who would pay you dearly to reveal it."

"Well, you'll probably always be 'Suit Man' first." Then she looked back up. "You were a rock and you probably saved my neck with David. If I had been alone he'd have made the evening unbearable. I really was dreading it before I met up with you downstairs. As it is, David will probably just whine over the phone tomorrow.''

"Yes, about that. I don't mean to get you into hot water with your agent. If you have any reservations about doing the work for the journals, just say so. Otherwise, give me a call.''

"Tomorrow?''

The suddenness took him back for a moment, but he quickly covered. ''Yes!'' he said a bit too eagerly, then in a lazier voice, ''That would be fine.'' He hastily dug his wallet out of the inside pocket of his jacket, than handed her his business card.

''I'm usually in the office pretty early. You can reach me there anytime after seven-thirty A.M., but you may want to wait until after eight—when I've had my coffee.''

Kate smiled. ''It will definitely be after eight before I crawl out from under.'' The elevator pinged and Edward's heart sank. He wanted the ride to last longer. He wanted her to volunteer her own phone number, but no such offer was made. He'd have to look her up in the tenant files at the office tomorrow morning.

''Well, good night.'' And she had backed off, then had turned with her key already in her hand.

The screen saver popped up on his computer, snapping him back to the present. The words *''Cyber Scribe''* popped out on the screen in three-dimensional–style lettering, then crumbled like dust into a little pile at the bottom of the screen to be swept up by a little janitor with a push broom. Edward switched off his computer and finished unbuttoning his shirt. Kate had as much as said what she thought of him. She had said that he was unapproachable. Certainly it was not possible to come to regard an unapproachable person as a close friend.

He switched off the light, then headed to bed to wrestle with his demons.

Kate sat back at her computer a little bit disappointed. She had wanted to tell someone about her evening and that someone had been Cyber Scribe, yet her friend had put an abrupt end to their conversation tonight. She supposed that was just the difference between men and women. Had it been a girl-friend she had been chatting with she would have asked for all of the details, but a male friend—and she entirely believed Cyber Scribe to be male—probably couldn't care less. She had deciphered his gender more from the little hints he gave away every time they "spoke." He may have even used some giveaway pronouns before, but she couldn't be certain. It had simply seemed obvious and his abrupt closing tonight was just another hint.

For the first time in their writing relationship she wondered if perhaps Cyber Scribe could be jealous. It had not occurred to her before that perhaps because of all they shared with each other over the Internet he might consider their relationship to be exclusive. That was something to think about and something to try to sound him out about the next time they chatted.

Kate sat on the carpeted floor in front of the computer monitor, a cup of coffee in one hand and her other arm wrapped around her knees. Her bare feet peeped out from under a long, flannel, threadbare nightgown and her hair was still tousled from sleep. Fritz the cat had made a nest for himself on some tracing paper beside her. It was a few minutes after ten in the morning.

"Cyber Scribe has entered the room."

Kate hastily uncurled, accidentally kicked the cat, then set her cup of coffee on the floor beside the keyboard.

DaVinci: Good morning, friend.

She switched to a privacy mode so no one else on the chat group could read their messages. Cyber Scribe did likewise.

Cyber Scribe: Good morning to you, friend.
DaVinci: Sleep well?
Cyber Scribe: Sleep? It's practically lunchtime.
DaVinci: What time zone are you in?
Cyber Scribe: The same one you're in. Only some of us begin our day a little earlier than others.

DaVinci: It's Sunday!!!
Cyber Scribe: I guess I might be considered something of a workaholic.
DaVinci: You're not the only one.

Kate thought about Edward. She was remembering correct. He had said that he'd be in the office this morning—at 7:30 A.M.!

Cyber Scribe: You working this morning, too?
DaVinci: I probably will doodle some a little later. Actually, I made arrangements to talk to someone about some work I'll be doing. I told him I'd call today, but I had forgotten it was Sunday. I guess I was just eager for an excuse to see him again.
Cyber Scribe: Lucky dog.
DaVinci: You never asked me about my date last night.
Cyber Scribe: With the "kook"? You gonna kiss and tell?
DaVinci: There was no kissing going on. I just wanted to let you know that. You ended our conversation rather abruptly last night. I was afraid maybe you were upset that there might have been—kissing, that is.
Cyber Scribe: This is a computer-generated recording— beep—I mean, would it matter to you if that mattered to me?
DaVinci: Well, of course it would matter to me. I don't figure two people spend half of their waking hours talking to each other and not feel at least some sort of commitment. Maybe this isn't the sort of thing you even want to talk about. Maybe you have a wife and kids, or maybe you're an international playboy who wants the stability of a female confidant that looks like a computer monitor. (By the way, if you have to picture me as a computer, think of me as one of those sleek, laptop models.) I guess I'm just asking if I should, in the future, keep my social life to myself, or if that's the sort of thing I can share with you.

There was a long pause before Cyber Scribe responded. Kate beeped him twice before he tapped out his own response.

Cyber Scribe: I don't want you to feel obligated to me in regards to limiting your social life. I'm happy to hear anything you care to share, but first consider sharing it with a real person.
DaVinci: You're not real?
Cyber Scribe: I suppose I'm both. The thoughts that I type are real, but you don't really know me. You don't know who I am or what I do or where I live. For all practical purposes I could very well have no body other than your computer monitor. I could be some sort of . . . "kook."
DaVinci: Oh, if only! I'll talk to you later. Gotta make a phone call.
Cyber Scribe: 'Bye, friend.

Kate felt a bubble of laughter in the center of her chest. It was as if she were sixteen again and she was calling the boy she had a crush on in high school. If Edward had half the wit, compassion, or intuitiveness of Cyber Scribe she could end her aversion to real-life romance and fall madly in love with him.

She was just reaching for the phone when it rang under her hand. She jumped, laughed aloud, then picked up the receiver.

"What is it with you, Katherine?" her agent began without the courtesy of a hello. "You seem to be constantly on the telephone. Your phone bills must be out of this world."

"And good morning to you too, David. I was on the computer. I know. I really should get a second phone line."

"The phone company should simply employ you. I would encourage it if your work hadn't enjoyed such a huge success last night."

Kate leaned back, resting her elbow on the carpeted floor. "David. A compliment? From you?"

"A well-deserved one. There were two purchases of your work made last night and three serious inquiries for commissioned pieces."

"That's fabulous." Kate sat forward with the good news. "But listen, David, I still want to do this science journal."

"Katherine, you don't need to do grunt work anymore. Don't you hear what I'm telling you, dear? You are an artist! Your work is in demand for something more than black-and-white slides for some high-school anatomy course."

Kate smiled inside, but she dug in her heels. "First of all, it's not slides for a high-school anatomy course. It's illustrative work for what is going to be a well-respected science journal. I want to be in on that. And second, I'd be flattered to do the work for any high-school science course."

"You're all heart, Katherine, but we'll have to discuss this at some length first. Toward that end, I was wondering what you had planned for tomorrow night."

"Tomorrow night?" Kate saw looming ahead of her another night of talking with the artistic elite. "Er, nothing. Why?" she asked warily.

"I thought we could have dinner together. You name the place. I'll pick you up at, say, ᴄeven?"

"Who do I have to impress tomorrow night, David? I don't think I'm up to another evening of introductions to complete strangers or chitchat with people who know more about art history than I could if I had lived through it."

David snorted on the other end of the line and, as if he were in the room, Kate could picture the upturn of the one side of his lip. It was the only sort of smile she had ever seen on his face. His full smile he reserved for wealthy art partons.

"Just me, Katherine. We're due a victory celebration. You left so hurriedly last night with your sugar daddy I didn't have time to tell you what a success the evening been."

Kate bristled. "My 'sugar daddy,' as you refer to him, is a neighbor and the gentleman for whom I will be working." She cringed at her own choice of words. While Edward was every bit the gentleman, calling him that only made him seem as old as David implied that he was.

"I understand, Katherine. Don't get your dander up, but we will have to discuss the direction your work is taking. I'll pick you up then at seven tomorrow."

"All right, David. Seven o'clock."

They both hung up simultaneously and Kate sat staring down at the clunky black telephone cushioned on the thick pile carpet. Just when Kate thought she had her agent figured out, David Tipton did something completely out of character—like this.

Again, the phone rang and again Kate jumped.

"Hello?"

"Hello, Kate. Edward Tucker here. I just wanted to let you know that I've decided to take the rest of the day off. I know you said you'd call later today to discuss the journal project, so I just wanted to let you know where I could be reached."

"Good morning, Edward." There was still sleep in her voice although she had been awake for nearly forty-five minutes now. "I'm glad to hear it. I was beginning to fear for your social life."

He chuckled. "Well, you could help me toward that end. How about lunch with me? We could talk out on the terrace."

The fabled terrace apartments. Kate was dying to see one of them. She had ridden the elevator to the twentieth floor before, but there wasn't much difference between that hallway and the corridor on the sixteenth floor. However instead of six apartments, there were only two. They must be massive.

Kate's apartment wasn't small and it cost her a fair penny, but her curiosity over the layout of the terrace apartments was enough to make her decision for her. She told herself that was the reason butterflies did somersaults in her stomach.

"I'd love to meet you for lunch."

"Great! Is noon too early?"

The thought of eating anything before two in the afternoon turned Kate's stomach. "Noon would be fabulous. I'm starved."

They rang off and Kate jumped up from the floor where she had been seated. She had a lot of spit-and-polishing to do if she wanted to look anywhere near presentable before noon. She ran to the bathroom and switched on the bath tap, then pulled out her toothbrush while the bathtub filled.

Kate stood outside the door to Edward's apartment. Her hair glistened; she wore an unaccustomed splash of pale pink lipstick, and an off-white dress that was conservative in the amount of skin it covered, yet flirtatious in the way it hugged her curves.

"One, two, three," she whispered to herself. She took a deep breath, then pressed the doorbell. A shrill buzz could be heard from the inside—not at all the sort of dainty doorbell she would have expected in one of the terrace apartments.

She bit her lip when the door wasn't answered right away. Was she early? No. She was never early. Maybe he had had to step out for a moment? Was she at the right apartment? She looked to the other end of the corridor, but the only other apartment entrance was blocked by a large box labeled LIGHT FIXTURES.

Finally she heard someone fumbling around on the other side of the door, then it was suddenly pulled open.

"Hi, neighbor. Come on in." Edward wore a kitchen towel around his waist like an apron and he held a basting brush in one hand. Some sort of barbecue sauce ran down the handle and he caught it with his other hand before it blobbed onto the floor. He looked down just in time to miss tripping over some two-by-four scraps. "Just watch your step. Everything is still a bit of a mess inside. I'm doing some renovations."

Kate looked around the apartment wide-eyed, then said exactly what she was thinking. "Edward, this place is a wreck!"

He laughed and waved for her to follow him.

She did have to watch her step—very carefully. Lumber was piled to one side of what would eventually be the foyer. Gypsum board was stacked against one wall in the living room; all of the furniture, save for one recliner and a television, was pushed to one wall and covered with a dropcloth. Wires dangled from the ceiling where a light fixture would go and a thin layer of sawdust and dry putty dust coated the wooden floors.

Kate stepped over a long flat open box full of the pieces for a gas log fireplace. "This is definitely not what I expected."

"You were expecting marble and tapestries?" He stopped at the double French doors that led outside to the terrace and turned to face her with a grin.

"Well, maybe not exactly all that, but . . ." She looked back over her shoulder at the obstacle course in his living room, "I did suspect that you were a bit of a fussbudget."

"Come on out." He waved her on and disappeared around a large potted tree.

It was outside that Kate caught her breath. The terrace was a veritable jungle of potted plants. To the right was a solarium. The open glass door revealed a potting bench, a porcelain sink, and a neat stack of terra-cotta pots below. A row of orchids lined a long table that ran down the center of the room, and various seedlings sprouted from low trays on the shelf below. From the ceiling, hooks held hanging baskets of flowering plants. In all, the greenhouse offered more variety than most nurseries.

Straight ahead was a view of the park and beyond that, the cityscape. The view was framed by potted trees on either end of the terrace and smaller concrete pots of low, creeping plants around a wrought-iron bench. The bench was covered in an invitingly thick, striped cushion that beckoned visitors to sit and enjoy the view over their shoulder.

To the left was where Edward had disappeared. The five-foot side walls of the terrace were hung with potted plants, except for the section around a large outdoor cooktop/grill. There, two racks of ribs sizzled and Edward lavished another coat of barbecue sauce on them. An iron table, prettily arranged with flowers, striped placemats to match the chair cushions, and cobalt blue dinnerware was situated on a low dais to gain the best views while eating. Toward this end, the two chairs they would be sitting in for lunch were both pulled to one side of the table.

Kate, finding a bowl with a half-peeled cucumber there, took her seat and began cutting the remainder of the vegetables that would go in their salad.

"I stand corrected. This is beautiful. Everything and more than I had imagined."

He smiled over his shoulder, then turned and wiped his hands on the front of the towel. "I've renovated the rooms I use the most first. The kitchen is serviceable, as well as the master bath and bedroom. The others I rarely ever use, so I saved those rooms for last. Unfortunately, you've gotta walk through those rooms to get to these. My poker pals told me I'd have to finish the den before winter. They're tired of having the cards blown out of their hands.''

Kate laughed. She had not imagined Edward sitting around the iron table with his male friends playing poker. That was supposed to be done in somebody's smoke-filled kitchen. ''You play poker? Now that I've gotta see.''

He pulled another paring knife from the drawer under the cooktop and took the seat beside her. He was wearing a shortsleeve polo shirt and jeans. ''We play Tuesday nights if you're game. I have to warn you, though, it's penny-ante with a nickle cap and these fellows are serious about their losses. You could stand to lose, oh, I don't know, one, two, maybe as much as five bucks a night.''

Again Kate laughed, then handed him the tomato that lay beside the bowl of salad. ''It sounds like great fun. Are you sure the fellows wouldn't object to the intrusion of the female element?''

''I don't think that'd be a problem, considering one of the 'fellows' is named Claire.''

Kate sobered slightly, but didn't allow it to show on the outside. She had not considered the prospect of Edward having a girlfriend. But why wouldn't he? He was certainly in his prime. It would be most unusual for him not to be married or at least have a regular in his life.

''The game is held at my place every other Tuesday, but Ned is laid up with a broken foot so it won't come around again for three weeks, but we'd love to have you.''

Kate's heart fell. Anything could happen in three weeks. He could become engaged to his poker pal, Claire, in three weeks. Maybe they already were engaged. ''I'll have to bone up on my poker rules, but I'd love to come.''

''Great.'' He dropped tomato wedges on top of the bowl of salad in front of her, then picked up a carrot and began scraping it onto his plate.

Over a lunch of salad, baked potatoes, and spareribs, they discussed the work for the journal. The articles had already been reviewed and chosen for the first issue. On Monday morning, Edward would contact the editor of that department who usually handled the arrangements for lining up the artists for the cover work and give her Kate's number as a contact.

"Here. Let me write it down for you." She looked about her for her handbag, then took from it a pen and a small scrap of paper. She wiped her barbecue sauce-stained fingers on the linen napkin, then stopped abruptly.

"Please don't wash this with your darks." She held up the napkin, then folded it and placed it back in her lap.

"Well, of course not."

She looked at him skeptically over the ink pen which she had taken into her hand. "You say that, but I've seen your laundry habits. Downstairs? In the laundry room?"

Edward nodded. "Ah, yes, I've since come to learn the error of my ways. You see, my washer was on the fritz." He pointed over his shoulder toward some room which must house his washer and dryer. "I'm afraid I had let the laundry pile up until the repairman could come and when he didn't show up for the second appointment, I rather took it out on my laundry by doing some speed washing. You know, everything in one load on one temperature—hot."

"And the result?"

He nodded. "Pink and lavender underwear. I've learned my lesson." And he took a bite of a sparerib. "But *you* have a washer/dryer hookup in your apartment. Why are you still using the laundry room in the basement?"

Kate put down the pen and sipped at her glass of ice water. "Furniture," she gave as explanation once she had taken the cobalt blue glass from her lips.

"Furniture?"

"Furniture. I don't have any."

He scowled and put down his rib. "You don't have any furniture?"

"Nope." She directed her attention to the piece of paper on which she jotted her phone number. "Oh, I have a mattress, a computer, and an easel, of course, but no sofa, no chairs, no washer or dryer."

"Is this some sort of artistic thing?"

Kate laughed. "Like wearing black clothes or painting to Mahler? No." She had never really thought about her reasons for not replacing her old stuff. The final decision in her moving from her old place and getting away from the stalking exfiancé had been his invasion of her apartment.

One night while she had been out, she had neglected to lock a bathroom window. He had entered the bathroom and proceeded to vandalize and destroy everything that had made her life comfortable. Family photos had been destroyed, her sofa had been de-fluffed with the stuffing pulled from its coils, lamps and vases broken, nearly every piece of kitchen glassware destroyed. The building she had lived in went undisturbed while her apartment alone had been completely trashed. When she had returned later that evening she had felt completely violated. She had had to wake a neighbor to call the police since her slimline phone had been smashed. It was a wonder that no one in the building had called the police while the devastation went on, but no one claimed to have heard the disturbance. That had happened on the same day Kate had left her job with the magazine and she had never seen the exfinacé again.

She had never had the heart to replace her old furniture although she had renter's insurance. Instead, she had cashed the check and bought a monster computer setup, a new mattress and linens, and left the rest for a hired to cleanup crew.

Even her clothes had had to be replaced, as the vandal had seen fit to tear up most of what she owned. It was probably the most difficult time of her life. The police had been fairly unsympathetic, believing it to be some sort of domestic affair that would only get repeated a few months down the road. In the end, it had been her grandfather, Harry, who had helped her pick up the pieces by taking her in for the few years preceeding her success in the field. By plunging herself into the routine of her work as a freelance illustrator she slowly got over her ill-fated romance. She thought she had fully recovered, but she found herself unable to tell Edward the whole story.

"I lost all of my stuff in a burglary one time. I just never had the heart to replace something that could get lost again."

"Goodness." He seemed truly concerned. "You were robbed? When did this happen?" Instinctively, he reached out and touched her hand.

That strange flutter returned to her stomach and Kate welcomed his consolation. "Oh, it wasn't anything that happened since I've lived here. Besides, I think you're safe on the twentieth floor."

"Well, I hadn't imagined anyone had scaled the wall to the sixteenth floor. You . . . you weren't hurt, were you?"

"Oh no." She quickly alleviated his concern and shook her head. She took a quick breath and blurted out, looking down at his hand next to hers, "It wasn't actually a burglary. I don't know why I said it was. It was my ex. It seems another woman believed her relationship with him was equally exclusive. When I broke it off, he . . ." She shook her head, searching for the right descriptive. ". . . snapped. He broke into my place one night and trashed it. I haven't heard from him since."

That wasn't exactly a lie. She heard his heavy breathing over the phone several times afterward. Harry had had a listed phone number and her ex-fiancé had learned through the grapevine that that was where she was living after the break-in. He had made several more harrassing phone calls before they had had to get an unlisted number.

"I'm sorry." He moved his hand and Kate felt immediately deflated. She worried that perhaps she should not have told him that she had been engaged before.

She smiled, more than ready to change the subject, then picked up the piece of paper under her pen and handed it to him. "Here is my phone number. It's unlisted." He took the paper from her proffered hand. "Oh, and I should warn you, I'm almost always on the phone. You see, I leave my computer on while I work, which ties up my phone line."

"I know."

"Huh?"

"Er, I mean, your line was busy when I tried to call you earlier this morning."

"Oh." Kate was satisfied with his explanation. "Well, it's almost easier just to pop in when you come home from work. Here." She took the paper with the phone number from his hand and scribbled at the bottom. "16-C. There you go. When you come calling I can offer you a glass of iced tea, if not a chair."

"Thanks." He tapped the paper with his index finger. "But I already have your—number and address."

For an instant, a sick feeling swept over Kate and her distress must have been apparent on her face.

"From your application," he quickly answered her troubled look. "Your application for tenancy. You filled out one when you moved in and updated the phone number once it was installed." She still looked worried. "I have access to those files, because I own the building you're living in." He studied her face. "Didn't you know?"

Immediately, relief flooded her face. "No. I didn't know." She blushed. She had experienced that same feeling of invasion of the sort she had felt the night her ex-fiancé had vandalized her apartment. Immediately, she felt guilty for having suspected, even for an instant, that Edward might be capable of anything near what she had experienced in her last love affair.

"No. I'm sorry. I had no idea." She fell silent, tongue-tied.

Edward quickly helped her out of her embarrassment. "No need. I should have—would have—told you. But of course you wouldn't know. Most of your business must be conducted with the management company. No reason you should have known."

Kate cleared her throat uncomfortably, still feeling embarrassed for her mistaken assumptions where Edward's intentions were concerned. She tried to laugh it off. "Well, I'm happy to know you're not doing all this work"—she gestured with her hand toward the terrace—"on a building that doesn't belong to you."

He smiled and helped make a smooth transition in changing the subject. "So, are you sure I wouldn't be disturbing your work if I popped in tomorrow evening?"

She was taking another sip of water, but put the glass down to answer. "I work really odd hours. I take breaks to do my laundry, to watch a soap that I'm addicted to, and to play with the cat whenever the mood strikes me. Sometimes I work business hours, but it's just a fluke when I do. Usually, I work whenever the muse snags me—which is pretty much all of the other hours of the day.'' Then she remembered her previous engagement. "Oh, I almost forgot." She slapped her forehead. "I told David I'd meet him tomorrow night for dinner. He's picking me up at seven."

Edward raised a questioning eyebrow. "So it's a date?" Immediately, he shook his head. "That's rude of me. None of my business."

But Kate was already shaking her head. "No, That's perfectly fine. No, it's not a date. I think David felt guilty about being so rude last night. He said it was a victory celebration for my success at the opening, but I suspect he has ulterior motives. He wants me to categorize my work. He thinks a little food and wine will help dissuade me from taking any more illustrative projects, but that's a debate he simply won't win."

She didn't want to leave, but she felt she had compromised enough of his day. She had spent almost three hours in his company and she was content to stay on his terrace chatting the remainder of the afternoon, but Harry's advice haunted her. Company is like old fish—they both start to stink after three hours.

With a sigh she stood up and collected her plate.

"No. Leave that. I'll get it later." He also stood and pushed back his chair.

Hesitantly, she put the plate back on the table. "Then I'll just thank you for a fabulous lunch. I don't know when I've had better food. I don't know when I've *ever* had ribs before—probably never. They were fabulous." She wiped at the sauce stain on the front of her dress. "If not more than a little bit messy."

"My pleasure." He smiled down at her, then cautioned her with his hand to watch her step down from the table dais. "I'll pop in sometime tomorrow evening then, to give you any information our editor has on the first issues of the journal. You probably should talk to her or have your agent hash out the financial details."

He walked her to the door and she hesitated before stepping

over the stack of two-by-fours at the door. She was not quite certain how to leave things with him. As inappropriate as it may have been, she wanted to kiss him. He solved the problem for her by extending his hand at the door.

"I'm sure it'll be a pleasure doing business with you, Kate."

"If this is how you wine and dine all of your freelancers, then I'm looking forward to doing business with you often." She turned and opened the door. He also stepped over the lumber, then held the door for her. She moved toward the elevator, then looked back while she waited for it to respond to her press of the button. "I look forward to hearing from you tomorrow." The elevator doors opened all too suddenly, she stepped in, and then the doors closed and she was gone.

Chapter Three

Kate quickly turned the leg bone sketches into a painting. A wrinkled sheet was stretched across her dining area, and she studied it as the backdrop for the skeletal knee joint. It was an unusual piece and an unusual assignment. This particular piece had been commissioned by a major hospital to hang at the entrance of the orthopedics department. It had an abstract feel to it, done in muted whites, tans, and browns. It was a soft drawing which made the metal prosthetic hinge stand out as something revolutionary. It was no longer a human skeleton, but a cyborg.

Kate looked over at the digital alarm clock on the carpet by the door. It was nearly 5:30 in the afternoon and Cyber Scribe had been conspicuously absent from the chat group all day. She had tilted her monitor to point up toward the easel where she worked so she would not miss him, but he simply was not on-line.

"Fine, then. Be like that." She finally flipped her computer off with her big toe. Fritz the cat stretched and changed his sleeping spot from the corner of the dropcloth under the easel to the top of the computer. Kate was still grumbling about Cyber Scribe's avoidance of her when her doorbell sounded.

Immediately, she forgot about her computer pal and her heart fluttered. No one ever visited, meaning it could only be Edward. She jumped over the telephone, pushed the clock out of the way of the door, and swung it open without even checking the peephole.

"Hi." He smiled down at her without moving. She grinned back without offering to let him in, so he finally thrust out a business card. "The science editor's number. She was excited when I told her you were available to do the cover work."

Finally, Kate remembered her manners and took a step back, inviting him in with her hand. "Please, come in. Have a seat." She gestured toward the only pillow in the middle of what would be the living room floor.

"Amazing. You really *don't* have any furniture."

Kate closed the door and moved around him toward the kitchen door. "Only the essentials. It makes cleaning very easy. Now, about that glass of tea. Do you take sugar?"

"Yes, please," he accepted. Kate fumbled around the kitchen, but spoke to him from the next room while he milled around the living room. He walked to the easel and inspected the still-wet painting, then he turned to inspect the bare walls.

"I'm surprised you haven't put any of your work on your own walls."

"Heavens no," Kate called from the kitchen. The tea was already made and she quickly filled two glasses with ice. She put them on a tray, threw some prepackaged tea biscuits on a saucer, and returned to the living room. "Can you imagine staring at somebody's dissected brain through dinner? Or how about a blowup of liver cells hanging over your mantel? It's just not pretty stuff. I can't imagine why anyone would want to purchase it as art."

Edward pointed toward the easel. "I can well imagine hanging this in the den. It's like. . . ." He considered the analogy. ". . . like those sketches by Leonardo da Vinci. You know—the ones of his inventions? Especially the sketch of the man with wings—sort of half-human, half-machine—bionic."

Kate smiled. That was precisely what she had been aiming for. Never used to open praise of her work, however, she blushed and wanted to change the subject.

"Come on. I'll take you on the grand tour." She set the tray of tea and cookies on the rug, glared at Fritz as a command to leave it alone, then moved toward the open door to the right of the kitchen. "This is probably pretty silly to show you around your own apartment." It still struck her as funny that he owned the building. "I haven't done much to improve upon the floor plan. This"—and she turned on the switch by the door—"is the bathroom."

He brushed her arm to squeeze into the small door beside her. Everything was precisely as it had been when she had moved in, without the addition of curtains or rugs. A white towel hung on the chrome towel rack and a clear, plastic shower curtain hung on the rod over the bathtub.

"Yep. Pretty much standard issue," was his comment with a grin.

Kate laughed. Seeing it through his eyes was really quite funny. It was as if she had intentionally chosen the few personal touches to blend into the background. "And this"—she moved out of the doorway, crossed the living room to the left side of the kitchen, and turned the doorknob there—"this is the bedroom."

Slightly more had been done to this room to make it more welcoming. For the two windows over the head of the mattress, Kate had invested in custom-made Roman shades—again, in white. The mattress, which took up the center section of the floor, was covered in a matching off-white on white-striped brocade comforter with matching shams. On the beige wall-to-wall carpeting that ran throughout the apartment, it all posed a fairly bleak environment.

Edward poked his head around the door frame to take it all in. He stepped back and looked at the living room again. The one pillow in the middle of the floor was the only spot of color in the room save for the orange cat that sniffed the tray of tea and cookies.

"Scram, beast." Kate walked to the tray and gently scratched the cat on his head, pushing his nose away from the cookies.

Again, she invited Edward toward the oversized needlepoint tapestry pillow and she made herself comfortable, facing the pillow and moving the tray between them.

Still in a smart, double-breasted business suit, he was not prepared for roughing it on the floor. He unbuttoned the front button and gingerly lowered himself to the pillow. He was still looking around the apartment as if to take it all in.

"What?"

He laughed. "I'm sorry. I know I'm being nosy, but you told me you were addicted to some soap on television. Where is your television hiding?"

Kate jumped up and ran to the kitchen. She returned with a small hand-held television, the size of a telephone receiver. "Ta-da."

He took it in just one large hand and gently turned it over as if he had just traveled through a time machine and had never seen a television before. "You decadent fool, you."

Placing the television on the floor beside him, he leaned back on his hands, then nodded toward her computer setup in the corner of the dining area. "So, you're computer literate."

Kate glanced over her shoulder, then took a sip of her tea. "My social life."

"Your computer?"

"Yeah." She put her glass of tea down on the tray as the carpeting made it too unsteady on the floor. "My best friend lives in that little box over there, only we've had a bit of a falling-out recently. I think he's not speaking to me today."

"Not speaking to you? What reason could you possibly give someone to not speak to you?"

"Believe me. It's possible." Kate smiled, feeling less anxious about being cut off from contact with Cyber Scribe so long as Edward was around. "You see, I work alone all day, so I turn to some chat groups for human company. I think my Internet friend was scared off when I got too personal the other day." She shrugged. "But no matter. He'll come around in time."

"He sounds like a boyfriend."

Kate smirked. "That's what he's afraid of, I think. It's one thing to share personal thoughts over the Internet, but once it begins to look like you might have to reveal yourself as a real person, a lot of people are hesitant. I mean, you lose the shield of anonymity." She glanced back over her shoulder toward the computer. "I'll let him baste a while. He'll come around."

"Well, if he's afraid of meeting you he must be some sort of kook."

Kate's head snapped up and she looked hard at Edward who

was absorbed in choosing a tea cookie. "Scary," she whispered, shaking her head.

He took a bite of cookie, then continued, looking up but not noticing Kate's startled reaction.

"The other night when we first arrived at your opening, I thought, just for a moment, that perhaps you and your agent . . ."

Kate laughed, putting aside what he had just said that had made her do a double take. "David? Now that would be a match made by the devil himself." She shook her head. "David's type runs more toward the blond and buxom."

Edward's eyes traveled from the top of her brown hair to the pink-painted toenails at the bottom of her slim-fitting blue jeans.

"Besides, I think I've learned my lesson where that sort of thing is concerned," she continued, unaware of his inspection. "I will *never* get involved again with someone I work with."

Edward nodded thoughtfully. "No. I can see how that could cause problems."

Suddenly, she looked up again. "So, tell me. What's your story,"

"Well"—he stretched out his long legs to the side, making himself comfortable for his tale of love and misadventure— "I fell in love with someone I worked with." He smiled fondly, then shifted his gaze from the carpet to Kate. "We both had Mrs. Pinkerton for algebra in high school. We married before I was even out of college—against everybody's better judgment—and we remained married for fifteen years— against everybody's bets. She died three years ago."

"Oh, I am terribly sorry to hear that, Edward. I had no idea." She looked down at her glass of tea. "Tell me when I should butt out. I seem to be making a habit of asking personal questions these days." She was thinking about Cyber Scribe who, for all their sharing, had never revealed even half of what Edward just had.

Quickly, Edward shook his head. "No. Not at all. I don't mind sharing these things. Besides, it's good to talk about it." He glanced down at his watch, then started to stand. "And talk with you all evening is precisely what I'd love to do, but

I see it's getting on to be six o'clock. Your agent will be here soon to pick you up for your victory celebration and you're not even dressed yet.'' He brushed the wrinkles out of the front of his pants, then rebuttoned his coat.

Kate looked down at her paint-spattered pants, then realized she must look as if she needed a lot of dressing up to be presentable. She was never very neat when she worked. She stood up, wishing she had changed before so they could go on talking up until the moment her agent arrived. She was sorry she ever accepted David's invitation to dinner. She knew he was cooking up something and after her abandonment by Cyber Scribe, she did not feel up to dealing with her agent.

''Well, maybe we could continue this conversation another time,'' she hinted, but he did not bite. Instead, he took the tray of tea things from the floor and moved toward her kitchen.

''Oh, don't bother with those, Edward.'' But he had already taken them into the kitchen. That room was as Spartan as the rest of the house and he shook his head with a chuckle.

''Amazing.''

She smiled and followed him to the door. ''I'll call the science editor tomorrow morning sometime.''

''Good. She's eager to talk to you.'' He pulled the front door open, took the three steps to the elevator doors, and pressed the button. ''In the meantime, give your Internet buddy another chance. Maybe he just had to be away from his computer today.''

Kate held up her hand in good-bye, then slowly closed her door between them as the elevator pinged and the doors opened.

He had been on the verge of telling her that he was Cyber Scribe, but some weakness in him would not permit the words to escape his lips. Why, he berated himself, did he ever suggest commissioning her for the work on the journals? If she was truly opposed to a romantic relationship with men she worked with, he wouldn't jeopardize his Internet relationship with her. Certainly, he reasoned, it could not be wrong to continue at least one of his relationships. Yet, a platonic relationship over the Internet was a poor substitute. He felt awful as he rode up on the elevator to his own, lonely apartment. As he turned the key in the door and walked in, he wondered who was the greater mess: he for all of his messy renovations or Kate for her denial of comfort?

It was no mystery what the root of his problems were. He was attempting, in a physical way, to put his life in order. The year spent caring for his wife before her death had turned his entire life upside down. The chaos of his apartment was merely a physical reflection of his emotions. He and his wife had always been ''in like'' with each other. He had made the most of his marriage and when she had left him for someone else, he had felt cheated. He had not recognized that they both deserved more. When she came back announcing that she had terminal cancer, he had used it to prove to her that he was there for her ''for better or worse.'' They endured the ''worse'' together.

After her death, he was left feeling like a man without a purpose. The daily demands of caring for an invalid had been all-consuming. Guiltily, he felt as if his task had been accomplished in seeing to her comfort to the end.

Slowly, he was putting meaning back into his life. It had begun with the daily grind. He had been in a position, financially, to enable him to take time away from his publishing house. When he finally returned to the office he realized how much the business had suffered for his inattention. He threw himself into the trade full force. When he came home in the evenings, he had thrown himself into renovating the terrace apartment he had taken as a single man when his wife had left him.

It was not until two days ago, speaking to Kate on the terrace, that he realized what he had been doing over the past several years. He was building a life for himself designed toward catering to his own comforts. One room at time, beginning with the master bedroom, he had geared his attention to the minute details. He had become an accomplished finish carpenter, obsessing about the new trim work and plaster detailing. As he had completed a room, he added order to his new life.

Part of that new life was revealing more of himself, first to his computer pal, DaVinci, then later to DaVinci's real life counterpart, Kate. Via computer he told her about the nuts and bolts of his daily grind. When he encountered something either fascinating or annoying at work, the first person he told was DaVinci. In a weird sort of way, he missed being able to tell his computer friend about his latest interest in one of his tenants, Katherine Delaney.

He found himself able to talk to Kate about the one event of his life that he had not been able to share with DaVinci. He never spoke of his marriage over the Internet. Eventually, he knew he would reveal everything to Kate about his previous marriage. There was time for that.

She would probably learn most of the details from the people who had known him and his wife as a couple. During the separation and following reconciliation most of their friends had blamed his wife and thought it selfish of her to return to him just because she had needed him. To Edward, that she returned was never a problem. That she had left in the first place was the problem. He recognized that they had married too young and that their marriage, while not an unhappy one, had never been a blazing success. They had had little in common to begin with and less by the time his wife had left him. It was not until the diagnosis of advanced cancer that they had reconciled and he had moved back into their home in the suburbs. Their last days together had been sweet and he would never regret them.

While thoughts of Kate and her evening with her agent raced through his head, he did not realize he had removed his coat, rolled up the crisp, white sleeves of his dress shirt, and picked up the sledgehammer that had been leaning against the living room wall. The first slam rattled the front door on its hinges. He swung again and broke a hole through the wall into a small closet. He thought about Kate and her hand-held television. This niche would make a perfect entertainment center that would inconspicuously house a big-screen television.

Kate looked out the window of the lobby and impatiently tapped her foot. David was not more than fifteen minutes late, but she resented it just because she was not looking forward to their evening together. When at last brakes squealed out front, she did not need the sight of his green roadster to confirm that it was her date. She rushed out the door as he saw fit to park in a no-parking zone. It was always his own convenience that was important to David. His eagerness for his own comfort realized itself in the sizable commissions he earned from his clients' work. That was probably why he was such an effective agent.

David was out of his car and bouncing up the steps to the apartment building when Kate met him halfway.

"Aren't you the dear. Right on time."

Kate smiled halfheartedly. "I wouldn't want to keep you waiting," but she secretly thought if the evening started early it would end the same way.

"I thought we could have drinks first, then dinner?"

"Actually, I don't drink." He turned a raised eyebrow toward her, so she answered, "I work and live alone. Drinking's not a good habit to develop."

He shrugged and moved around his roadster, not bothering to hold her door for her. She did not expect it, however. They were not on a date.

Fifteen minutes later found them seated in an upscale restaurant. David ordered a drink before his meal arrived, with Kate's permission, and then he lowered the boom.

"Now, Kate, I want you to withdraw from whatever handshake agreement you have with your sugar daddy to do those illustrations. They can only hurt your career."

Kate bristled. "First of all, you can stop calling him my 'sugar daddy.' You won't win any points with me by continuing. I am very fond of him, but that has little to do with my decision to do the cover art for his journal."

"Forgive me, Kate, but I think your feelings for this man are muddling your perception of your work. If you continue to think like an illustrator, that's all you'll ever be. No one is going to accept you as a true artist if you continue to attach your name to hack work."

"Thanks a lot, David."

"You know what I mean. It's dull, grinding labor."

"Yadda, yadda."

He reached into his breast pocket and thrust out a check at She took it tentatively, then nearly spewed her water across the table.

"This check is made out in my name!"

David smiled with assurance. "And just count those zeros." He sat back and took a sip of his drink. "That's for just one of the pieces that sold the other night."

"But I wasn't asking even half—"

"You weren't asking anything. I'm your agent. I have a feel for fair market value."

"Fair market? This is obscene." She giggled, then slapped a hand over her mouth.

"Now, will you trust me when I tell you what I believe to be the best direction for your work to take?"

Kate sobered. "I won't turn down this assignment. As far as taking on any others, well, you'll have to let me think it over some more."

Their food arrived, so Kate dove in. The faster she ate, the sooner she could end her evening with David. He turned sulky for a few brief minutes. It was during the main course when she felt him staring at her.

"What?" She wiped at her nose, certain she must have wine sauce on the tip.

David shook his head. "Oh, nothing." And he quickly looked back down at his own, untouched plate.

"Listen, David. It's not that I don't truly appreciate all of the effort you've put into advancing my career. It's just that, well, fame and fortune isn't the end-all and be-all. There's gotta be something more, something that gives your life meaning and purpose. Selling a painting for a five-digit figure isn't the sort of thing I can take a lot of pride in. Mind you, it'll buy a lot of cat food." She sliced through the chicken on her plate. "But what can I tell Harry when he asks what I've accomplished for the day?"

"Your grandfather, the philosopher. How is Harry?"

Kate looked back to her plate. "He's fine."

David leaned forward with elbows on the table and his chin on his intertwined fingers. "Has he still got that old sedan?"

The one time he had met Kate's grandfather, he had drooled

over Harry's car. It had been built in 1943, had less than 25,000 miles on it, and had been kept in a garage. It was in mint condition, but not because Harry obsessed over it with wax and polish every weekend. He simply did not think it was necessary to drive it the three blocks to the grocery store.

Happily, David allowed the conversation to be turned away from Kate's career for the remainder of the evening. Toward dessert Kate found she was even enjoying herself, but not so much so that she was not willing to leave when the check arrived. She offered to pay, feeling more than a little obligated with the enormous check she had secreted in her handbag, but David insisted.

She watched the side of his face suspiciously as they climbed back into his roadster. He had been awfully abrupt in dropping the subject of her career. That was not the David Tipton she knew. He would fight to get his own way. In fact, she could not remember an instance in their three years together when he had not gotten precisely what he wanted out of her. She had never turned down an assignment he had brought her way.

Back at her apartment building, he hesitated before climbing out of the roadster. "Listen, Katherine. I'm sorry about referring to your boyfriend as your sugar daddy. I, of all people, know you don't need someone just for their money."

Kate smiled her appreciation for his apology. "Thank you, David. I can't actually claim him as a boyfriend either." Then she added with a shy smile, "Well, not yet."

"Smitten, are you?"

She nodded. "I think he may turn out to be someone pretty special, but . . ." She hesitated and turned to look up at the front door of her building—Edward's building. "He really is just a neighbor. We'll see how things develop."

David finally moved to open his door.

"Oh no, don't feel like you have to see me to my door."

"At least let me see you inside the building."

Kate shrugged then climbed out of the car and headed up the few steps to the front door. It required a key to enter the lobby, which she produced from her handbag. David opened the door once she had it unlocked, then held it for her. She stepped inside, then turned at the door, barring his further entry.

"Well, thank you for dinner—and the check." She shook her head, still not quite believing it. "It was completely unexpected."

"It was *your* work that sold."

"It was *you* who set the value," she returned.

"And I wish you would let me guide you in the direction your work takes."

Here it comes, Kate thought to herself, but only smiled sweetly. "I told you I'd think on it awhile."

Just then, the elevator doors swished open and Kate looked over her shoulder in time to see Edward exiting. He wore dark pleated pants, the color of which was indescribable under the coat of white dust that covered the front. The sleeves of his once-white shirt were rolled up to his elbows and his hair was wet to the scalp.

"What the . . . what's happened to you?" She turned toward him.

"Kate." He was surprised to bump into her, and for all the mess he wore on his clothes, he wore a pleasant smile. He shrugged. "Who'd have thought there was a water line in that wall?" Then with that as his only explanation, he nodded a greeting to David Tipton, then moved past them both and left via the front door which David still held.

"Oh, dear."

" 'Oh, dear' is right. What a mess." Wet footprints were left where Edward had been. "Well, it's been a pleasure, Katherine, but you'll excuse me if I rush off."

Kate was startled by the abrupt exit. She had entirely believed that David had been waiting for her to invite him up to her apartment, but now he was leaving. He had not seen her apartment before.

"Yes. Of course, and again, thank you."

David nodded, then let the door close behind him. Kate watched from the door as he reached his car, then looked over his shoulder at her. She waited until he had climbed behind the wheel and started his engine, then she turned and boarded the still waiting elevator.

*   *   *

Edward moved at a steady pace. He hoped he was not going to get to the hardware store five minutes after it closed. He glanced over his shoulder. He was not usually spooked walking alone at night. Besides, he looked a fright. He could not imagine that anyone might approach him. If anything his appearance, if not his size, would scare off a mugger. He heard the sound of an engine racing. He kept walking until he heard a sudden downshift and felt, rather than saw, a car slow on the street beside him. He looked over, steeling himself for a confrontation with fists clenched.

It was David Tipton, Kate's agent. He slowed his pace, then stopped as the agent did likewise.

"Give you a lift?"

Edward raised his eyebrows in disbelief, then took the few steps to his passenger door. He made no move to board, but leaned on the edge of the door. From the way the agent looked at his grimy hands on the door, Edward thought he would regret having offered him a lift. Edward looked down at the spotless interior, then down at the front of his own filthy pants.

"Yes. That would be nice." And climbing in, he only barely got his seat belt fastened before the agent pulled out. "I was headed to the hardware store. It's about eight blocks along here." He pointed straight down the street where they were heading. As the agent made no attempt to carry on the conversation, Edward began. "So, did you and Kate have a nice evening?"

David shifted jerkily then glanced toward his passenger. "Lovely, thank you." He did not attempt to continue the polite conversation.

"So, I guess she told you she's decided to do the illustrations for the magazine?"

David nodded. "Yes. Against my advice."

"You really believe it will hurt her career?"

The agent shrugged. "It's not the direction she should take. Attaching one's name to that sort of work could be devastating to an artist's career."

"It's right up here." Edward pointed toward the shop with the barrel of brooms out front.

David downshifted, then braked to come to a screeching halt outside the store. Edward was surprised when the agent also unfastened his seat belt. "Mind if I tag along? I can give you a lift back to the apartment."

Edward raised a suspicious eyebrow, but said no more. Together they entered the store just as a young clerk was taking in the bucket of brooms. The shop was readying to close.

"Hey, Jeff," Edward greeted the teenager. "I won't be a minute." Then he headed toward the plumbing department. The agent was on his heels and Edward chuckled as he glanced over his shoulder. David Tipton looked like a fish out of water in his baggy black pants and oversized coat and knit shirt of the same color. "I'm looking for a coupling joint," he spoke over his shoulder as he rummaged through a wire bin of plastic pipe fittings.

"Actually, I didn't come along to look for plumbing accessories with you."

Edward glanced at the agent, then turned his attention back toward the second bin. "I figured there was some other reason."

"It's Kate. I just wanted to let you know she's still getting over a rough patch. She's very vulnerable."

Without giving him the courtesy of looking at him, Edward kept searching for his plumbing part. "I know. She's told me all about that."

"She has?" He sounded surprised.

"Well, of course she has. We're becoming pretty well acquainted."

"She's told you, then?"

Edward nodded and finally stood up straight to look the agent in the eye. He rested an elbow on an upper bin. "You sound surprised."

"Well, frankly, I am. She's told you about her . . . disappointment?"

"No, but why don't you fill me in? Something seems to be troubling you."

David Tipton shoved his hands deep into his pant pockets. "To be perfectly blunt about it, I *am* troubled. Katherine isn't usually this careless, but I suppose the separation has really thrown her for a loop.''

Edward's eyebrow shot up. ''Separation?''

David Tipton ran a nervous hand through his thick black hair. ''I was afraid you didn't know. Kate is married.''

''Harry,'' Edward said more to himself.

''Harry?'' David repeated. Then, ''Harry, yes, of course,'' the agent continued. ''She's mentioned him to you? You knew she was married yet you felt no qualms about having an affair with a married woman?'' As he spoke, his voice rose. ''Oh, I thought far better of you, Edward.''

Anger flushed Edward's cheeks. ''We're not having an affair,'' he said too loudly, and Jeff the clerk glanced down the aisle with interest. On a softer note he repeated. ''We're not having an affair and I sure didn't know she was married. Still married or ever married. She mentioned an 'ex'—I assumed she meant ex-boyfriend—and she said the guy had destroyed all of her furniture.''

David shook his head, suddenly sympathetic. ''Of course she doesn't have any furniture. Her husband . . .'' He hesitated. ''Harry got everything in the separation agreement. The house, the furniture . . .''

''Wow.'' Now it was Edward's turn to run his hand through his own hair. The dampness left it standing on end. ''I had no idea.''

''Well, thank goodness. I was afraid you knew and didn't care. As it is, I think Katherine can be forgiven. No one should have to go through what she's been through.''

Edward recalled how Kate had hesitated when telling him about how she had come to have no furniture, first telling him that her apartment had been burglarized, then telling him it had been destroyed by a vandalizing ex—he assumed boyfriend. He saw his hopes for finding love again go swirling down the drain. His wife might have left him, but she had always been honest about her reasons.

''Listen,'' David Tipton continued, ''I have no reason to tell you any of this other than a sincere wish for Katherine's happiness and safety. I hope you won't let on that I've spilled the beans.'' Then as almost an afterthought, he said, ''And I hope you won't hold it against Katherine. She's really had a hard year. I can't fault her for attempting to leave her past behind.''

Edward shook his head. ''No. Of course not.'' He began to feel guilty for being angry with her. After all, she had not given him any reason to believe that she wanted anything more than his friendship. In fact, she had attempted to dissuade Cyber Scribe from thinking of her as anything more than a friend by sounding him out on his feelings for DaVinci.

David Tipton left without providing the promised ride home, but Edward felt he needed the time alone in the fresh air to get his head on straight.

David Tipton squealed out from the curb. Kate would hate him—maybe even fire him as her agent if she ever found out what he had done, but he had not made himself the success that he was without a little backstabbing. He reasoned, however, that it had been for Kate's own good. Her involvement with this old man could never lend itself to her career as an artist. This Edward Tucker was far too conservative to be an artist's amour.

He had planned to tell Kate's sugar daddy that he and Kate were married, but that would have meant making up lies about a possible reconciliation and having to pop in on Kate occasionally. It was Tucker himself who gave him the brilliant idea of implicating Kate's grandfather, Harry, as the man to whom she was still married. Harry would certainly visit his granddaughter occasionally and perpetuate the myth that they were married instead of blood relations.

''Yuck.'' The agent voiced aloud his distaste for the association he had been forced to concoct, then he turned on his radio, cranking up the volume to a level that would drown out his nagging conscience.

Edward felt cheated. Why had DaVinci at least not told Cyber Scribe about some of what she must be going through? They shared every other minor daily annoyance. Why not the fact that she was in the middle of what sounded like a less-than-amicable divorce?

Edward threw the plastic coupling joint down on the counter, left a one-dollar bill and some change, then shoved it in his pocket and headed out the door. The manager smiled and said, "Good night." Edward did not respond. Absorbed in his own thoughts, he shuffled down the street the eight blocks back to the apartment building.

As he entered the lobby, he half expected/dreaded that Kate might be there or that he might bump into her on the elevator. He needed some time alone. Once upstairs in his own apartment, he set about the chore of repairing the pipe he had broken. He had been able to turn off the water at the stopcock at the base of the closet wall. The entertainment center niche seemed like a silly idea now and as soon as the plumbing repairs were made, he headed toward his computer.

He hesitated a moment, swore under his breath, then switched on the computer.

"Cyber Scribe has entered the room."

Edward was about to perform the search to see if DaVinci was on-line, but before he could type the command, he received his answer

DaVinci: Hey, friend. Am I in the doghouse?

Cyber Scribe: Is there anything you should be in the doghouse for?

DaVinci: I was beginning to wonder. I hadn't heard from you all day. I was afraid you were miffed at me for getting too personal.

Cyber Scribe: I don't think that's possible over the Internet. It's anonymous. You asked me before if I would object to your telling me about your social life. I'm all ears, or eyes, as the case may be.

Kate switched to a privacy mode, so that no one else on the chat group could read their messages.

DaVinci: I've met someone in my apartment building who I think I could really fall for. Mind you, we haven't

spoken above three or four times, but I don't know.
There's just something different about him and how we
interact. We connect—sort of like me and you, only
he's got a body.
Cyber Scribe: The kook?
DaVinci: Yeah! And the funniest thing . . . today when I
had tea with him that's what he called you.
Cyber Scribe: He called me a 'kook'? Under what
circumstances?
DaVinci: I told him I thought you were giving me the
silent treatment because I hadn't heard from you all
day. He said you'd have to be some sort of kook.

Seated at his computer, Edward rapped his forehead with
his knuckles.

Cyber Scribe: You said he was someone you could 'fall
for.' Is there any impediment?
DaVinci: Impediment? Does a person in love ever have
a choice in the matter?
Cyber Scribe: Do you know what love is?
DaVinci: Granted, I don't have a blazingly successful
track record where affairs of the heart are concerned.
I've been burned once, but he's not like that. I don't
think he could ever hurt me the way the other guy did.

Edward cringed at his own behavior. At first, he had felt
justified in rekindling his conversation with DaVinci because
Kate had lied to him, but what if she was just trying to leave
a hurtful past behind? What if the crazy story about the ex-
boyfriend had been the only way she could deal with the obviously hurtful behavior of her husband? Perhaps this Harry
fellow was half a bubble off-plumb and had trashed her first
place after they had separated.

He recalled his own separation. He had been so angry—
had felt so cheated by his wife's abandonment—some nights
he would drive by their old house just to watch the lights on
inside. He stopped driving by after the night he had seen her

through the living room window sitting on their sofa with her new boyfriend.

> *Cyber Scribe: I would only advise that you make certain*
> *you know what you want. Make sure this guy isn't just*
> *a temporary substitute for a lost love.*
> *DaVinci: I'm not even sure the feelings are mutual. He*
> *may have no interest in me at all.*
> *Cyber Scribe: He's male, isn't he? Men always have an*
> *interest. Just make sure you're being honest with him—*
> *and with yourself.*

And on that note, they both signed off for the night. It was getting late and Edward began to feel the strain of his renovations, work, and long hours. He wondered if he was getting too old for romance. He was definitely older than Kate.

As he undressed for a shower before bed, he looked in the mirror and sucked in his stomach. He wondered how old Harry was.

Chapter Four

Kate left the science editor's office, traversed the hall to the receptionist's desk, then made her way down the hall to the executive suite. It had been nearly two weeks since she had last seen Edward. Either he was making himself scarce because he really had meant only to employ her for the science journals, or he was very busy with his many different projects.

The door to his office stood open, so Kate didn't bother to knock. Inside, however, an elderly man sat at the desk in the center of what Kate supposed to be the receiving room. He typed using two fingers and his attention was held by the copy he kept looking to in between searching for keys on the keyboard.

Kate checked the inscription on the outside of the door to make sure she was in the right place. It read in small, nondescript type: V. EDWARD TUCKER. A nameplate on the desk, however, read: CLARENCE CAVANAUGH.

Clearing her throat got the old gentleman's attention.

"Pardon me." He turned away from his typing. "I didn't see you there, ma'am. How can I help you?"

"Sorry to break your concentration." She nodded toward the copyholder. "I was hoping to catch Mr. Tucker in."

The elderly man tipped his chin down to look over the top of his half-moon glasses at Kate. "Now, I hate to have to ask you this, seeing as you're so pretty and considering how that one in there"—he nodded toward an inner door—"ain't had the company of one like you in quite some time, but do you have an appointment?"

Kate tried to conceal her surprise and then the smile that

was trying to work its way out. "I'm afraid I don't. It was purely a social call. I had hoped I might talk him into having lunch with me."

The old man's eyes lit up and his bushy eyebrows rose to meet his thin hairline. "Well, then, that'll just have to be arranged." He pointed to the chair in front of his desk. "Now you just sit yourself down there and I'll get his appointment book." He produced a calendar from the top center drawer of his desk and opened it with a flourish. He found the day and time with his index finger, then picking up an ink pen, he licked the tip and made a sharp line through whatever had been written on the calendar at lunchtime.

"It seems an opening just came up."

"I don't want to bump somebody else who went to the effort of making an appointment with him." Kate had only just seated herself, but she sprang from her chair to leave.

"Now don't you pay no attention to that, Miss . . ." He fished for her name.

"Kate. Kate Delaney."

"Well, Kate Delaney, it's like this. If we don't help him along he ain't never gonna get back into the swim of things. Look here." And with another lick to the tip of his pen, he penciled in something on the next page. "He can see the property manager tomorrow. I'll ring 'em before they've had a chance to expect him, hardly."

Kate took her seat again. Just then, the door to the inner office burst open. Kate's chair was positioned at an angle, so Edward did not see her immediately.

"Clarence, what's on my calendar for today? I know there was something I was supposed to do at lunchtime, but I can't remember . . ." He trailed off. "Kate!"

She turned in her chair to look up at him. "Good morning, Edward."

"Oh, you came by to see the science editor?" He moved to stand beside her so she would not have to strain looking over her shoulder.

"I've just met with her and I think we've worked out most of the nuts and bolts. Your office has a pretty standard contract for commissioned artwork. Actually, I popped in to see if you'd be available to have lunch with me.''

He smiled suddenly, then as quickly, his smile faded. He turned to the gentleman whom Kate figured must be his secretary. "Where are my manners? Clarence, meet Kate Delaney. Kate, this is my good friend, Clarence Cavanaugh.'' Both parties stood to shake hands. "Now Clarence, didn't I have something on the book for lunchtime today?''

Clarence pointed to the crossed out reference. "You're in luck. The property manager has had to cancel." He gave Kate a wink. "You'll be having lunch with them tomorrow. You're free to have lunch with Kate Delaney today.'' He said it as if it were an order.

Edward held up his palms. "Looks like I'm free. Just let me grab my wallet out of my desk.''

Kate stood, leaving Clarence with an appreciative smile, then followed Edward into his office where he rummaged through his top desk drawer. He stood with his back to her, giving Kate an opportunity to reacquaint herself with his form. He was dressed for a day at the office in a dark suit and a necktie. The mere sight of him after two weeks made her nerves jangle. In one way she felt guilty for those sorts of emotions. Was she cheating on Cyber Scribe? Grabbing his coat from the back of his chair, he turned, then was startled to see that Kate had followed him.

Nearly tripping over his desk chair, he reached for his computer monitor and switched a button on the bottom of the monitor. "Don't want to burn up my screen while I'm away,'' he offered as explanation for his furtive behavior.

Kate was taken aback. He had been hiding something from her. He had not realized that she had followed him into his office and he did not want her to see whatever it was that was on his screen.

"Shall we?'' He gestured for her to precede him, then he followed her out the door. In the outer office, he turned again to Clarence. "What's next on my calendar?''

Clarence looked to the book still open on his desk. "Nothing until three o'clock. You kids have fun.''

It was not intended for Kate to see, but she did, nonetheless, as Clarence gave the thumbs-up and a silent whistle to Edward.

"So, did you get your water leak fixed?"

"Hmm?" Edward had been lost in his thoughts. "Yeah. That seems like weeks ago."

His mind was elsewhere and Kate wondered if it was back in his office with whatever he had felt he needed to hide from her on his computer screen.

"It *was* weeks ago. Two to be precise. So where would you like to go for lunch?"

He thought for a moment. "Trudy's?"

That hadn't been exactly what Kate had been expecting. She imagined them dining in a quiet, dimly lit restaurant. Trudy's was almost what could be considered a dive. She had been there once with her grandfather and it was a mostly male lunch counter.

"Not what you had in mind? We can go someplace else."

"Oh, no. Trudy's is fine. I've been there before."

"I go there a lot on business. It was just the first place that popped in my head."

So, he lumped their lunch date into the category of "business." "No. Really, it's fine."

"Okay. We can walk. It's just around the block." He made no effort to take her arm as he had at her art opening, but instead he only barely slowed his pace enough for her to keep up.

Kate had hoped they could make it a long lunch, but Edward was making that seem unlikely. Just around the block, Trudy's was tucked under a group of low-end lawyers' offices. As it was just before noon the real clatter of dishware had not yet begun. Luckily, Kate thought, one of the only two booth seats was still vacant. Edward seemed to hover toward the barstools, but Kate made a beeline for the booth.

Edward took the seat across from her, then noted, "Looks like we were just in time." A large party of men in business suits came in the door behind them. They looked to the booth, then made themselves comfortable at the bar that seemed to wrap around three sides of the small room. "Are you certain you don't mind eating here?"

Again, Kate reassured him. "I like Trudy's. I've been here before." She picked up a menu from the wire holder at the wall side of their table, then added, "with Harry." She looked up to catch his intent study of her face. "Have I told you about Harry?"

"You've mentioned him."

She only nodded as if that was all that needed saying before turning her attention back to her menu. "Seems everywhere I go, everyone knows Harry. He's quite the social butterfly. The day he brought me here, he seemed to know everyone."

"What does he look like? Maybe I've seen him here before?"

"Let's see." She laid down the menu and clasped her hands in front of her. "He's about my height, gray hair." Edward frowned. "He owns a dozen denim shirts—all of them look alike—and the only difference between his summer and winter attire is the occasional shift from denim to khaki. He turned seventy-six last July—"

"Seventy-six!?"

Kate looked at him quizzically. "Seventy-six." She smiled. "But he's very fit. He's probably most easily recognizable by his car."

"Does it make you uncomfortable being here now?"

Kate puzzled over his question. She looked around at the all-male clientele and decided that was the reason for his question. "Because of the male presence? Not at all. It's one of Harry's favorite hangouts when he comes into town. Oh!" She thrilled at the prospect. "I'm not expecting him, but what if Harry should come in today? I could introduce you to him."

A scowl stood out on Edward's brow. "I don't think I'm prepared for any sort of confrontation."

Kate laughed. "Well, he's not the confrontational sort. That's a funny idea." She put her menu back in the rack, having made her choice.

Their conversation drew to a standstill as Edward perused the menu. When he snapped it closed, he looked up to find Kate studying him intently.

"You're looking very serious, Suit Man."

He tried to smile, but failed. "So, how long were you and Harry together?"

A waitress came to their table, interrupting Kate before she could answer. They both placed their orders and were left with two glasses of ice water.

"Three years, six months, and two weeks, but before that, we practically lived together." Edward's left eyebrow rose. She continued, "My parents lived in a house on his farm and I was as often up at Harry's as I was at home. It was later, after my parents died that I moved in with Harry." She turned somber, distractedly squeezing lemon into her water. "Actually, I only lived with him during the holidays from college. He was always great about making me feel like that was my home, too."

"I'm sorry, Kate. I didn't know."

She shrugged. "How could you? I hadn't told you until now." She smiled again, all reserve gone from her face.

"I gather that you and Harry haven't completely severed your ties."

Kate shook her head. "Well, no, of course not. Certainly we don't see as much of each other as we used to, but he's still my only living relative."

"And that's why you still think so highly of him? You don't live with Harry, but you're still pretty attached to him."

Kate frowned. "Of course I'm attached to him, but he doesn't decide my every move anymore." She took exception. "It was simply time to leave the nest, I suppose. It was never supposed to be a permanent arrangement. Anyway, it's hard living with someone else—especially Harry. His expectations of me are greater than David's. With Harry, you eat, drink and sleep his philosophies on life. I'm too bohemian to live with Harry." She was feeling defensive. It was almost as if Edward was on David's side—trying to make her less dependent on Harry. "You'd love him. You'll have to meet him sometime. Then you'd understand why I rely so heavily on him still." She pushed her glass away. "But that's enough about me. I want to hear about you?"

Sitting back in his seat, Edward shrugged. "Well, there's not much more than I mentioned before. I was married for fifteen years. I considered marriage to be a lifelong commitment and when she died three years ago, I wasn't quite prepared for that commitment to end.''

''That's a long time with the same person.''

Edward flared. ''It's supposed to be a long time.'' He looked around the restaurant guiltily and Kate was taken aback by his reaction. He must have loved his wife very much, she supposed. ''Marriage isn't just a convenience that you enter into with a temporary understanding.'' He took Kate completely by surprise by adding, ''With me, I went into it as a lifetime commitment. I just never thought a lifetime could be so short.'' He took a sip of water, then made an effort to change the subject. ''I should mention to you, I bumped into your agent the other night. He gave me a lift to the hardware store.''

She was happy to change the subject. He was obviously still very emotional when discussing his dead wife. ''David? When was that?''

''When I bumped into the two of you in the lobby—after your date.''

''Well, it wasn't exactly a date, Edward. He was only giving me his usual song and dance. 'Focus on art for art's sake. Think like an illustrator and that's all you'll ever be.' Well, I don't find that disquieting.''

Their lunch arrived and Kate readied her napkin in her lap while the waitress placed the blue-plate special before her.

''So, what did you and David find to chat about? I never really thought of you and him getting along. I hope he didn't harass you about my work.''

Edward looked up from his plate. ''Actually''—he hesitated—''we talked about Harry.''

''About Harry? Well, don't believe everything you hear. There is no love lost there. Harry took an instant dislike to David the only time they met each other. You see, Harry has an old, classic car that David would give his eyeteeth for. Harry's only concern is that it can get him where he's going. Harry's a very pragmatic man who doesn't have time for what he considers silly and wasteful hobbies.'' Kate laughed and picked up her fork. ''He about had a hissy fit when I told him

I was studying art at college. It took me a month to explain its usefulness to society."

"You still think a lot of Harry, don't you?" Edward's smile was almost sad.

"Of course I do. Harry helped me pick up the pieces on more than one occasion. I wouldn't let a few eccentricities hamper my feelings for him."

"What do you think Harry would say about our having lunch together?"

Kate smiled shyly. So did he think of their lunch as a date? "Oh, he'd approve. You're actually quite a bit alike."

Shaking his head, Edward turned his concentration to his own plate. "I just can't see it." Then he murmured under his breath, "Seventy-six." A moment of silence ensued with Kate waiting for him to explain before he surprised her with an apology. "I'm sorry I've been scarce for the past couple of weeks. I've been very busy, both at work and working on the apartment. I'm hosting another poker party though. Are you game?"

Enthusiasm for the invitation was written all over Kate's face. "You know I am. After your last invitation I went out and purchased a computer version of poker. I've been practicing and saving my pennies."

"Good. It'll be this Tuesday at seven."

"Fabulous."

They finished lunch in companionable conversation discussing the latest in computer games. Kate promised to loan him her copy of the poker game and they agreed that he would walk back to his office alone after seeing her safely to the subway.

Edward returned to the executive suite, as always, filling the room with his presence. Clarence looked up from his desk. Edward knew the older man would have no qualms about asking his friend and employer any number of personal questions about his lunch date, so he took the chair Kate had earlier occupied and waited.

"Well? Why haven't I heard tell anything of that young one?"

Edward shrugged. "There's nothing to tell really. She lives in my apartment building. We met on the elevator and she's doing some artwork for the new science journal."

Clarence nodded knowingly. "And you like her."

"I like her, but . . ."

"But? There ain't no buts. Go for it, boy."

"But," Edward reemphasized, "she's much younger than I am. She has an aversion to mixing business and pleasure, and . . ." He hesitated, deciding to skip his whole deception of Kate about his Cyber Scribe identity, then he dove in, "She's still in love with her husband." It was important to Edward that Clarence approve of her. He valued the older man's opinion.

"Husband?! I'd say that was a bit of a snafu. What's she doing meeting you for lunch when she's got herself a husband? I swear, people these days just ain't got no sense of commitment. I'm sorry I cleared your calendar for her."

"It's not like that." Edward immediately defended Kate's honor. "They're separated. The best I can make out, he cheated on her—not once, but several times. When she left him, he stalked her and broke into her apartment. He destroyed everything she owned and I get the impression she's hiding from him."

Clarence sat back in his chair, steepling his two index fingers under his chin. "And you think she's still in love with him? She seemed like a bright-enough girl. You sure?"

Edward stood up. "I'm not sure of anything anymore. I thought I believed in lifetime commitments no matter what, but I'm just not sure anymore." He moved toward his office door. "I plan on finding out for sure though before I make a fool out of myself." And with that, he went to his desk, turned up the brightness on the computer monitor he had hastily switched off when Kate had followed him earlier, then took his seat.

The words *"Cyber Scribe"* danced across the screen saver. He impatiently tapped a pen on his desktop and waited a full thirty minutes, only occasionally wiggling the mouse so the screen saver wouldn't come up again.

"DaVinci has entered the room."

He pounded out a message on his keyboard.

Cyber Scribe: You're back. How'd your appointment go?

DaVinci: Very well, thank you. I had a nice lunch date, too.

Cyber Scribe: Don't tell me. With the kook.

DaVinci: Yes, with the kook, You sound jealous.

Cyber Scribe: Of the kook? No way.

DaVinci: Well, maybe you should be. He's beating your time.

Cyber Scribe: "Beating my time?" That sounds like something an old man would say.

DaVinci: It's a line I picked up from an old man. In an effort to be fair, I just wanted to let you know, the opportunity does exist if you'd like to go out to lunch sometime.

Cyber Scribe: How will I recognize you?

DaVinci: I'll be the only laptop computer wearing a red carnation in my port.

Cyber Scribe: I'm not sure I'm ready for that sort of exposure just yet. Things may be picking up in my own social court.

DaVinci: Now, I think I'm jealous. Who is the cheap CPU?

Cyber Scribe: You'd like her. I think you're a lot alike although she may be interested in me as only a friend. You see, she's married.

DaVinci: YIKES! Say it ain't so, friend.

Cyber Scribe: You have a problem with that?

DaVinci: I'm not the one with the problem. You're gonna have a major problem on your hands if her husband finds out.

Cyber Scribe: They seem to have an open relationship. They're separated.

DaVinci: Does there seem to be much chance of reconciliation? Are you prepared to stand in the way of a lifetime commitment between two people?

> *Cyber Scribe: Well, that's why I'm not certain where I stand in the scheme of things. She still seems to think highly of her ex even though he's cheated on her before.*
>
> *DaVinci: Maybe you could sound her out a little more loudly before committing to her. She could be sending out signals she doesn't really mean to send if she's still confused about her husband.*
>
> *Cyber Scribe: And how are things transpiring between you and the kook? Are you committed to him yet?*
>
> *DaVinci: I'm still holding out for you. All joking aside though, I'm serious about meeting you for lunch sometime. You just name the place and date.*

Edward grabbed up his pen and tucked it behind his ear, then swiveled his chair to face the window. This could be it, he thought. He could set a deadline for himself to confess to Kate and by setting up a date with DaVinci, he'd be forced to eventually tell her who he was. He called to the outer office.

"Hey, Clarence, what sort of evening obligations do I have in December?"

There was a delay, then the secretary called back. "The week of the fifteenth looks free. You want me to pencil something in?"

Edward hesitated. "Yeah. Just write me out—on a date."

He swiveled back around to the keyboard.

> *Cyber Scribe: December fifteenth, the Flaming Flamingo on Brewery Street. Have you ever heard of it?*
>
> *DaVinci: Heard of it!? That's in the city where I live!!*
>
> *Cyber Scribe: Surprise, surprise.*
>
> *DaVinci: You knew? You know where I live?*
>
> *Cyber Scribe: You must have mentioned it one time. Is it a date?*
>
> *DaVinci: You bet. How will I recognize you?*
>
> *Cyber Scribe: I'll be the only computer geek in the place.*
>
> *DaVinci: Just three months. I can hardly wait.*
>
> *Cyber Scribe: See you then.*

Outside of Edward's door, Kate jangled the cup of pennies she held in one hand while she balanced a plate of lemon squares in the other. She rang the doorbell with her elbow. Inside the apartment, Edward looked around to give everything one final inspection, then he threw open the door.

"I know I'm early. I apologize. I apologize. I was just excited about our poker date."

"Come in. I'm glad you're the first one here." He held the door open to her, relieved her of the plate of lemon squares, then waited for her reaction. He wasn't disappointed as Kate took in a quick breath.

The terrace apartment she had expected the first time she visited Edward was before her. Marble tile filled the front foyer and the walls wore a fresh coat of pale peach paint with white trim.

Kate took the few steps into the living room and looked around in amazement. Here the pale peach was repeated and the wood floors had been pickled a lighter shade than the oak's natural color. Where bare wires had dangled from the ceiling before there hung a brass chandelier with peach-and-white-marbled glass globes. What the room lacked in furnishings, it more than made up for in attention to detail. Crown molding circled the room and on the wall where Edward had broken a water pipe, he had installed a discreet entertainment center, the doors of which, when closed, concealed the new television inside. Edward's ratty recliner looked very much out of place in front of the gas log fireplace.

"This is absolutely fabulous."

"And this doesn't smell half bad either." He sniffed the cakes.

Kate looked back to Edward who had been holding his breath while she assessed the finished product. "So this is what you've been so busy doing."

Edward grew self-conscious. "I can't take all of the credit. My friend, Claire, has been giving me a lot to help. She's an interior decorator and I realized the place needed the feminine touch. She helped choose the color and light fixtures. Besides, it's getting too cold to play poker on the terrace. I had to bring the game inside." He gestured toward the dining nook. There, the only piece of truly nice furniture stood. A round oak table with claw feet was centered in the area atop a blue-and-peach Persian rug. Four fully upholstered light blue chairs surrounded the table with two more chairs off to the side. A slightly more formal chandelier hung from the plaster molding over the table. In the dining area, as in the living area, the walls were bare.

Edward put the plate on the table and Kate noticed the decks of cards.

"I thought we could play here, until I can find the right sort of game table to put in the living room."

"I can't think of anything you could have done to make either of these rooms any nicer." Kate smiled. "Except perhaps some furniture. I thought your furniture must be in storage while you did the renovations. Why haven't you got any or are you trying to copy my decorating style?"

He moved past her to the kitchen, then once inside, he opened a sliding stained-glass window between the two rooms so they could more easily talk. "I left all of the furniture at my wife's house when we separated. During her illness, I moved back into her house, but most of the furniture was sold with her house."

Kate sat in one of the cushioned dining chairs and distractedly shuffled one of the decks of cards. This was the first she had heard about a separation. It gave her something more to mull over.

"I plan to refurnish, but I'm in no hurry. Besides, I'm not really certain I know what I want. Functional, yet a little bit dressy. Definitely comfortable. My friend, Claire, has some pretty definite ideas about color though."

Kate looked around her. "Something with character. The rest of your place has character. Your furniture needs character, too. Maybe a mixture of antiques and new pieces?"

"Exactly. Maybe you could help me pick it out some weekend."

Kate saw another opportunity to spend time with Edward without actually taking the risk of asking him out. "I know just the place. It's a little antique/junk shop near Harry's place."

Edward looked up through the window dividing his attention between Kate and the stack of cold meats he was placing on a plate. "Harry?"

"I think you'd like this place. I used to go there a lot, when I was actually furnishing an apartment."

"Why don't you?"

"Why don't I what?"

"Furnish your apartment? We could go together and you could begin by purchasing something for your guests to sit on."

Kate smiled. "You didn't like my pillow?"

"Your pillow was lovely."

"Thanks. I made it myself."

"Now see?" He disappeared behind the wall, then came out of the kitchen door holding the plate of sandwiches. "That's just the sort of thing I mean. It's elegant, yet practical. I want to fill this place with that sort of thing. Perhaps you really wouldn't mind giving me a hand in choosing some furnishings."

"I've said I would, but I'm not sure you'll agree with everything I have to suggest." Her eyes traveled to the chair in the living room.

He already knew where she was heading. "You're thinking of my recliner."

"Actually, I was."

He laughed, then moved toward the foyer as the doorbell sounded. "Claire hates it too. It's about lost its comfort. I think I'm ready to part with it, but I have to first find a replacement."

He disappeared around the corner leading to the foyer, then threw open the door. "Welcome to Chateau Tucker!"

Kate smiled. He was enjoying showing off his new digs. She stood and remembered her nervousness when the first of Edward's poker buddies rounded the corner.

"It's about time you spruced the place up a bit," a familiar male voice was saying.

A lady entered the living area, her back still to Kate. She was tall, elegantly graceful and while she had taken great pains with her makeup, Kate thought she could easily be about ten years older than Edward. She was pulling off her sweater as she looked around the newly renovated apartment.

"I knew it would be nice judging from what you had done out on the terrace, but I have to admit, this is beyond my expectations."

Edward, followed by Clarence, entered the living area. "You know you just about gave me my marching orders the last time you were over for cards. It was either finish it or risk losing you." Edward leaned in to give the woman a kiss on the cheek. Kate wondered, was this the married woman he was interested in?

It was with Edward's lips still pressed to her cheek that the woman finally noticed Kate standing quietly in the dining area. Edward seemed to remember she was standing there and moved to introduce her.

"Kate, I'd like you to meet my dear friend, Claire Cavanaugh. Claire, meet Kate Delaney."

Kate stepped forward and extended her hand as the other woman seemed frozen.

"How do you do?"

"How do you do?" Claire repeated with curiosity.

"And of course, you know Clarence Cavanaugh."

Kate remembered the elderly male secretary. She also recognized that both Claire and Clarence had the same last name. He stepped forward to take Kate's hand, then surprised her with a kiss on the cheek. So only she could hear, he whispered into her ear, "You've got him, Kate. Just reel him in."

When he pulled away he grinned. Her face felt warm and she knew it had gone crimson.

"Now, what will it be to drink for everyone?" Edward started toward the kitchen, then did an about-face as the doorbell rang again. "Clarence, maybe you could help the ladies."

More voices filled the foyer and after the same amount of praise for Edward and Claire's handiwork, two men rounded the corner, one of them on crutches. The man on crutches almost immediately flopped into the recliner in the middle of the room.

Clarence fumbled around the kitchen and Claire joined the group in the living room, leaving Kate to stand hovering alone.

"Let me see this infamous broken foot." Claire first accepted another kiss on the cheek from the man wearing a cast from knee to toe, then knelt beside him.

"Kate, let me put you through introductions one more time." This time, Edward walked to where she was standing and took her arm to lead her toward the party.

"Tucker, you ugly cuss. Where'd you find this one?" The man in the recliner moved forward in his seat and extended his hand toward Kate. Kate smiled, taking an instant liking to all of Edward's friends.

"Ned Mackey, meet Kate Delaney. Kate lives in this building. We met on the elevator."

Kate smiled, releasing Ned's firm handshake.

"And this is Roland Samms." Kate accepted the fourth man's handshake, then enjoyed another kiss on the cheek. The apartment seemed to be immediately filled with the jovial conversation of close friends. Kate was accepted into the group and made to feel like one of the gang with Roland taking her arm, leaving Claire to assist Ned and his crutches into the dining area.

There, Ned removed his own lightweight coat and looked around for an appropriate place to hang it. Feeling like a hostess, Kate accepted it, then relieved Claire of the sweater she was still carrying on her arm. She glanced around for an appropriate place to hang the coats, but found none. There was no closet in the foyer and Edward certainly did not possess a coatrack.

It was Claire who pointed her in the right direction. "Oh, Tucker usually just tosses our things on his bed."

Kate nodded, then making herself at home she made her way down the darkened hallway that led away from the living area.

Kate did not need to find a light switch in the hallway, but groped with her free hand around the first door she came to. A flick of the switch revealed a freshly puttied and dusty room. The far wall was lined with windows and she knew, when Edward got around to renovating it, it would be an impressive sight with full southern exposure. She flicked off the light and proceeded down the hall.

It was the second door that revealed the room she sought. It was the master bedroom and Edward had spared no expense in seeing to his own comfort there. Beyond a small reading area lined with full bookshelves, columns separated the sitting area from the sleeping area. A king-size bed was centered on the exterior wall. Two dark wood night tables were positioned on either side. A thick pile carpeting cushioned the floor in this room.

Kate took a tentative step into the room, then with more assertion, she walked through the reading nook. The space invited her to sit, but she moved through the two columns into the sleeping area and laid the sweater and coat on the foot of his bed.

A door to the left of the bed led, Kate assumed, to the master bath. Turning back toward the doorway to the hall, Kate took in the highboy on the wall to the right of the columns and a tasteful rolltop desk to the left. It was here that Kate did a double-take. A computer was seated on the desk. The screen danced with a familiar name: *"Cyber Scribe."*

At first it barely registered, then her heart pounded. She walked up to the computer and touched the screen, but as if it had been a figment of her imagination, the screen restored itself. She had accidentally bumped the desktop with her thigh and the movement was enough to jostle the mouse, clearing the screen saver.

The window beneath the screen saver was familiar enough. It was the chat group she logged onto half of her waking hours. Kate's heart raced and without feeling as if she was committing any breach of privacy, she pulled out the swivel chair in front of the desk and pulled out the keyboard tray. She typed: *"Who am I?"* When she hit the ENTER button on the keyboard, the message she anticipated appeared on the screen.

Cyber Scribe: Who am I?

Her stomach did a somersault.

Transmutator: Are you going existential on us, Cyber Scribe?

Kate did not respond. Instead, she pulled the rolltop down on the desk. It explained a lot. For example, it explained how Cyber Scribe had known what town she lived in. It explained his hesitancy in meeting her in person. She thought back to her discovery of the chat group. She had learned about it when she had worked for the magazine. It was a publishing-related chat group, so it only made sense that Edward would be involved in it. But how, she wondered, had he been able to figure out who she was based on her name, "DaVinci"?

She pushed up the rolltop again and pounded on the keyboard.

Cyber Scribe: Hey, Transmutator. Is it possible to determine the true identity of someone on the chat group?
Transmutator: You just "finger" them.
Cyber Scribe: What do you mean?
Transmutator: I mean, you type "finger Transmutator" and you'll get a link to my name, address, and electronic mail address. However, Transmutator is no dummy. I have encrypted my identity. You will only meet my virtual self.
Cyber Scribe: Again, what do you mean, "virtual self"?
Transmutator: Unless you want any weirdo on the group to be able to identify who you are and where you live, you should encrypt your identity. You can create a fictitious identity for the fun of it. Didn't you download the "read me" file? It's all explained there.
Cyber Scribe: Thanks, Transmutator. It's been very educational.
Transmutator: And you've been very entertaining. I just fingered you. That's a pretty funny virtual self you've created, Cyber Scribe.

Kate pulled down the rolltop again and pushed the keyboard tray back under the desk top. She had not protected herself with a virtual identification, so it had been easy for Cyber

Scribe—Edward, she reminded herself—to find out who she was. How long had he known? she wondered.

Cyber Scribe had said that his social life might be picking up, but that the woman was married. Who had he been referring to? Certainly not her. Claire? Claire was married, but to Clarence. They did not behave like a separated couple. Certainly Edward would not consider stealing his friend and employee's wife.

Kate remembered she had been gone for some time, and, hastily, she made her way back out into the hall, remembering to switch off the light on her way. When she returned to the living room, everyone was just taking their seats around the dining table. Clarence was in the kitchen, but Edward had disappeared.

"So, where has Edward run off?"

Ned nodded toward the French door which led out to the terrace. "He's gone out to grab some more glasses off of the shelf out there."

Claire looked up from the cards she was shuffling. "So, Kate, how long have you known Tucker?"

"Not very long." It felt like a lie. She had been conversing with Cyber Scribe for the past year. They shared everything—except the real details of who they were.

"Well, here's what I'd like to know," Clarence entered the conversation from the kitchen serving window. "Just what are your intentions toward our man, Tucker?"

"Clarence, what sort of question is that?" Claire scolded.

"You'd have me pussyfoot around the good stuff all night and we'd be no more the wiser when we left than when we came. I want to know what she thinks about him."

Kate looked from Claire to Clarence, then took the seat between Roland and the vacant chair that Edward would occupy. "Oh, it's all right, Claire," she reassured the other woman. If Claire was the woman to whom Edward had formed an attachment, Kate wanted to find out if it was mutual.

"My intentions are clear enough," Kate answered. "I plan on marrying Edward." She finished to stunned silence. She looked around the table and everyone had stopped what they were doing—shuffling cards and counting out pennies—to stare drop-jawed at her. There was little difference between Claire's stunned silence and everyone else's. "Only he doesn't know it yet, so don't let on just yet awhile."

Just then, Edward opened the terrace door. "What's going on?" He balanced six cobalt blue tumblers on a tray, then turned to shut the door with his elbow.

"Hot dog!" Clarence clapped his hands with such a crack that Edward nearly dropped the tray of glasses.

"What the devil?" Edward scowled at his friend, then traversed the distance to the dining area and only just managed to put the tray on the table without dropping it.

Kate gave Clarence a glaring look that warned him not to spill her secret. Instead, he answered, "I'm just ready to play cards tonight."

The jovial air more than returned to the room. Edward took delight in the fact that his friends were so warm with Kate. If their friendly acceptance of her was anything to go by, he knew he had not made a mistake in setting his sights on her.

Chapter Five

"**P**ass those little lemony things down here," Roland ordered from the end of the table. "You're a lucky cuss, Tucker."

Again, Kate glared at one of Edward's friends to vouchsafe her secret.

"To live so close to Kate," he finished. "She's a darn good cook." He took a bite out of the lemon square and winked mischievously at Kate. She knew she would regret having said anything about her intentions before the evening was through.

Clarence reached into his shirt pocket and produced a crisp cigar.

"Now, you just put that thing away, Clarence," Claire scolded. "You're not gonna go stinking up Tucker's new place. Besides, that's why I don't live with you anymore. You stink up the whole place when you light up."

Kate made a mental note about their having once lived together. So they were separated.

"Aw hush," he complained in return. "I'm just chewing on it. I wouldn't light up without going out on the terrace."

"Nasty habit," Claire harped.

"Deal 'em out, Ned," Edward interrupted the two and smiled at Kate as he took the vacant seat beside her.

As the evening progressed, Edward's friends seem to take greater delight in harassing Kate about her declaration at every opportunity. It was Claire who struck a blow which all of the friends cheered.

Sending Edward after a drink refill for her from the kitchen, she turned conspiratorially to Kate.

"Perhaps you could answer a nagging question for us all." Roland, Ned, and Clarence seemed to lean in toward the table a noticeable inch. "We're all dying to know what the 'V' stands for at the beginning of his name."

Kate was prepared as Edward stuck his head through the kitchen pass-through. "What are they telling you, Kate? Don't believe a word they say."

Edward dashed back into the dining room, certain he had missed something.

"As a matter of fact, I *do* know what the 'V' stands for." She saw Edward out of the corner of her eye as he waved his hands, signaling for her to keep his secret. "I think one of the things that first interested me in Edward were his many little secrets. At the same time, I believe one of the things he saw to admire in me was my ability to keep those secrets."

Everyone leaned back with audible disappointment.

"Jerked the rug out from under our feet is what you've done," Roland complained. "Just remember, girlie, we have the goods on you, too."

Edward looked from one friend to the other, but no one was going to tell.

For the rest of the evening, the group of friends seemed to enjoy themselves and their respective secrets. It was getting close to midnight and Ned was happy to line his pockets with about half of everybody's pennies. Roland complained. "This man whines that he can barely walk, but look at the spring in his step when he leaves the table a winner."

Edward slapped Ned on the shoulder. "That was a good game, friend."

"Tucker, you just remember to bring this young lady with you to my house next Tuesday." Ned nodded toward Kate. "She takes her losses like a real riverboat gambler."

"The pleasure was all mine," Kate returned.

"Oh, I almost forgot." Ned stopped at the door and turned back toward Kate. "I'm leaving without my coat."

"Yes, of course." Kate moved away from the departing group and started toward the hallway.

"I can get it," Edward intercepted her. "Where'd you put your coat, Ned?"

"I didn't. Kate took it for me."

Edward shot a startled look toward Kate, but she met his look with a calm smile. "I laid both Ned's coat and Claire's sweater on the foot of your bed."

Edward's stomach made a sickening lurch. Had he left his computer on? He tried to be relaxed in his step, but he raced down the hall to his room, flew through the columned reading area, and turned toward his desk. The rolltop was pulled down, concealing the computer monitor, and he gave an audible sigh of relief. It was not usually his habit to pull down the rolltop, but he supposed he had done it in anticipation of Kate visiting.

More leisurely, he picked up the sweater and light coat that lay on the foot of his bed and made a mental note to change his screen saver.

In the living area, he smiled to see Claire leaving Kate with a warm embrace.

"Thank you for the encouragement, Claire," Kate was saying as he returned. When Claire looked up to see Edward she released Kate.

"You hang on to this one, Tucker. She's a winner," Claire enthused.

Kate tried to gauge Edward's reaction, then was swept up with another kiss on her cheek from Roland. "Lovely meeting you, dear. I hope to be seeing a lot more of you."

Edward turned to help Ned on with his coat and Kate enjoyed another embrace from Clarence. Edward strained to hear what the older man said.

"You come by the office again—soon. We have some things to discuss."

Edward helped Ned by holding one of his crutches while the other man maneuvered into his barn coat. As soon as he was attired, he took his crutch and hobbled toward Kate, planting a kiss on her cheek. "I'm planning on you coming next week, so you make sure you save your pennies and catch a ride with Tucker. He knows the address." Looking over his shoulder, he winked at his friend, then turned and extended his hand. "Tucker, I love what you've done with the place. Sure beats playing outside in the smog."

"Like I told Kate, I can't take all the credit. Claire here"— and he draped a casual arm around the woman's shoulders— "she picked out the paint and saw to it that I stuck to the same colors." Claire stood on her tiptoes to kiss his cheek, then turned to Clarence. "You two drive safely." Edward shook the older man's hand.

En masse, his friends left suddenly, leaving Kate and Edward standing in his doorway, in every way looking like a couple seeing their guests off for the evening.

"Thanks, Edward. I really enjoyed meeting your friends."

"Thank *you,* Kate. You were a real trouper and I hope the guys didn't embarrass you. They've made their own assumptions and I'm afraid they can be rather blunt at times."

But Kate was already shaking her head. "Not at all. They were all lovely." Still, her cheeks were a slightly brighter shade of pink.

Because she was standing in the open door, Edward assumed she was preparing to leave. In some ways it was easier to say good-bye without his friends looking on, but in another way, it put more pressure on him. With everyone leaving, exchanging kisses with Kate and Claire, it seemed the thing to do. Now that they were alone the onus was on him to decide if it was appropriate to kiss her or not.

Kate made the decision for him. Before he had quite decided how it should be done, Kate stood on her tiptoes and put her hand on his shoulder. He thought for an instant she was going to kiss his lips, but at the last second, she diverted her aim and kissed his cheek.

"Good night, Edward. I'll talk to you again—soon."

He only nodded, but held the door open, watching her until she was on the elevator and the elevator doors were closed.

In her own apartment, Kate raced to her computer.

"DaVinci has entered the room."
DaVinci: Finger "Cyber Scribe."

On Kate's computer appeared:

Weary traveler, you have traveled far to reach the humble abode of Cyber Scribe. As you enter, you must stoop your head so as not to bump it on the ceiling of my cave. The stalactites hang at odd lengths, forcing you to contort your body to enter. Inside, you see the warm glow of a fire. It takes a moment for your eyes to adjust, but slowly you make out the hunched form of Cyber Scribe. I sit holding a small clay pot of red paint in my left hand as I write on the cave walls. Come and join me, friend, and add your handprint to the wall.
DaVinci: Finger "DaVinci."

Kate's full name and electronic mail address appeared on the screen as well as her city of residence.

"Cyber Scribe has entered the room."

"You didn't waste much time," Kate whispered to herself.

DaVinci: Hello, my friend.
Cyber Scribe: Hello, DaVinci.
DaVinci: Well, I did it.
Cyber Scribe: Did what?
DaVinci: Kissed the kook.
Cyber Scribe: You should get that put on an apron.
DaVinci: Cute. And how is your love life? Picking up?
Cyber Scribe: Funny you should mention that. Things are looking up on my end, too.

Kate held her breath and held on to hope.

DaVinci: With the married woman?
Cyber Scribe: Yes.

Her heart sank.

DaVinci: Did you kiss?
Cyber Scribe: She kissed me—but only socially. A discreet buss on the cheek.

"Darn." Kate remembered Claire leaving and planting a kiss on Edward's cheek. Her encouragement toward Kate left her in no doubt as to the one-sided sentiments. Perhaps Edward was enamored with Clarence's wife, but it was merely friendly attachment on Claire's side. "I should have kissed you on the mouth," Kate swore under her breath.

DaVinci: So, what's preventing you?
Cyber Scribe: Other than a husband?
DaVinci: I suppose there is that, but you seemed to believe that she and her husband were separated—permanently. Other than this supposed attachment, what's preventing you?

She wanted him to admit to himself that he could never steal another man's wife.

Cyber Scribe: I think she has an aversion to mixing business with pleasure. It seems she had a bad experience once.
DaVinci: You never mentioned that you work with this woman. What does she do?

There was a long pause before he responded. Kate wondered if she had been mistaken about his affection for Claire.

Cyber Scribe: She's doing some painting for me.

Kate rapped her fist on the carpeted floor. She remembered he had said that Claire was an interior decorator and that she had helped him to choose the paint and some of the fixtures for his apartment.

DaVinci: You could always fire her.
Cyber Scribe: Now, there's a winning way to begin a
relationship.
DaVinci: Okay, maybe that's not the best way to begin.
So, explain this social kiss that wasn't a real kiss.
Cyber Scribe: You would have me kiss and tell?
DaVinci: Don't trust me enough to give up all of the
sweet details?
Cyber Scribe: I trust you implicitly. Just let me hold on
to some secrets.

"*Some* secrets? I'll say you've got some secrets." At the same time, she felt flattered that he trusted her "implicitly." She would help him to see that falling in love with another man's wife was a no-win situation. Kate held onto the hope that perhaps, in time, he could come to find some small amount of affection for her.

DaVinci: Very well, then. You hold on to your secrets.
Some day I'll confide all of my secrets to you.
Cyber Scribe: Are you keeping secrets from your old
friend?
DaVinci: A whopper.
Cyber Scribe: Fair enough. I make the same promise,
friend.

Kate wanted to say more, but her nerves were on edge. It was going to be hard to continue her relationship with Cyber Scribe and not let on that she knew he and Virgil Edward Tucker were one and the same person. She also wondered how long it would be before one of Edward's friends told him about her declaration.

The only positives were that she had found out, with a fair amount of certainty, that Claire was not as enamored with Edward as he was with her and that Kate had the full support of his friends.

Kate signed off for the night, then switched off her computer. She wandered around her empty apartment. Fritz caressed her leg and reminded her that she wasn't alone.

Although it was after midnight, she knew that sleep would elude her, so she did not try. Opening the easel, she set up a fresh canvas, then pulled out her brushes. It would be a house-warming gift for Edward.

Kate held the telephone receiver away from her ear. Harry had no problems with his hearing, but her grandfather believed a long-distance phone call meant the person on the other end was farther away, thus needed to be yelled at through the mouthpiece.

"He's a great guy, Harry. You'll like him."

"It ain't that agent fellow? I don't care for him one bit. He's got nothing better to do than take a fat chunk of your hard-earned money and stand around shining up his car."

"No, it's not David. This fellow's name is Edward. Edward Tucker, and he has plenty of worthwhile hobbies. Lately he's been renovating his apartment."

"Ain't nothing but a waste of time, renting an apartment. You sink all that good hard-earned money into a place and for what? You ain't got nothing to show for it in the end. You've just been taking care of somebody else's property."

"He owns it, Harry."

"What? One of them con-do-miniums?" He pronounced the foul syllables as if they were three words. "Darned fool investment. You sink all your money into what ain't much more than a treehouse in somebody else's tree. Somebody come along and tear out the floor below you and your house caves in."

Kate laughed. She knew Harry was being obstinate just for show. "No, Harry. He doesn't own a condominium. He owns the whole building. He's quite well-to-do." She said it knowing that would not have any positive effect on Harry.

Harry snorted. "How old is this fellow anyway? What does he do for a living?"

As if owning an apartment building wasn't enough, Kate thought. "He's in the publishing industry. I'm doing some artwork for one of his journals."

"He paying you?"

Kate's shoulders drooped. "Of course he's paying me. Listen, Harry, if you're going to be negative, I'm not sure I want you to meet him. He's a very nice man."

"Aw, don't go getting all defensive. I'll meet your young man." Then, "you didn't say how old he is."

"Ah"—she hesitated—"I'm not really sure. I've never asked, but I'd guess somewhere in his late thirties to early forties."

She could almost see Harry shaking his head. "You don't think he's a little bit old for you, girl?"

"No, Harry."

"How long you known this fellow?"

It was the inevitable question and Kate dreaded answering it.

"Just a little over a month." She felt like it was a lie and she could never get away with lying to Harry. He always had a sixth sense about her omissions and embellishments. "Like I said, we live in the same building, so we've known *about* each other longer than a month."

Harry hesitated. Then he announced, "I think I'll be coming into the city 'fore too long. You got room to put me up?"

"Overnight?" Kate was surprised. Harry had never stayed overnight with her before. He had an aversion to staying in any bed other than his own. "Of course I can put you up, Harry. When do you think you could come?"

His response startled her. "How's about tomorrow?"

Kate blinked at the phone. She fully understood his desire to check out her latest love interest. Considering her first and only engagement had ended so horrifically, Harry probably wanted to do a full background search on Edward.

"Listen, Harry, you're not going to ask him any embarrassing questions, I hope. He and I are really still just getting to know each other." She decided it was best to leave out the part about Edward being in love with his friend's wife. "We haven't committed in any way. I entirely believe he only thinks of me as a friend—nothing serious."

"I'm leaving my shotgun at home, Katherine."

Kate giggled. "I'd appreciate that. Do you need directions to the apartment, or do you remember the way?"

"I ain't senile. I can get through the city on my own."

Kate cringed. "Sorry, Harry. I didn't mean to imply that you were. Just be careful. And Harry?" She paused. "I love you."

Kate knew the old man well enough to know his lips would turn up at her words. "I love you, too, Katherine."

Kate hung up. She knew it was better to introduce Edward to Harry sooner rather than later. Harry had to be taken in small doses.

Kate paced from the kitchen to the front door, checked the peephole for the umpteenth time, then stalked back to the kitchen. She had been unable to reach Edward on the telephone to invite him to dinner, because, like herself, he was always on the computer. In the end, she had slipped a note under his door. She had not heard from him all day, so she could not be certain he had even seen her invitation to dinner. Harry would be arriving any minute and she really wanted a few minutes alone with Edward, if for no other reason than to prepare him. He would not be aware from her brief invitation that there would be anyone else dining with them.

Kate switched off the oven and opened the door, then jumped when the doorbell sounded.

"Oh, please, please, please, be Edward."

Kate's phone had been ringing busy all day and the few times he checked his computer, he had done a search to see that DaVinci was on-line. It was no wonder she had had to slip her invitation to dinner under his door. Her telephone was always tied up—much like his own.

Edward put an oven mitt over his hand and pulled his famous apple pie out of the oven. He wanted to see Kate too badly to wait until the appointed time of her invitation to dinner, so without even taking the time to cover the pie with anything, he strode out of his apartment and pressed the button on the elevator. It took more than a few seconds to arrive and oddly, when the doors did open, a man in a flannel shirt, a much-worn corduroy jacket, and jeans was standing in the elevator. It was uncommon to see anyone on the elevator when embarking, because in order to arrive at the twentieth floor the passenger would have to have that as his destination or have failed to press anything.

Edward nodded curtly. The man did not seem to pose any threat as he was much older, but wearing a floral oven mitt and carrying a pie did not lend itself to the appearance of someone who could hold their own against a mugger. Edward stepped into the elevator and turned to face the doors.

The older man rummaged through his breast pocket, then his rear pants pockets for something. It was in his front pants pocket that he finally produced what he had been looking for. He held a small scrap of paper in his hand close to his face, then at a distance, as if he was having trouble reading whatever was written there. Having finally deciphered it, he reached to press the desired floor, but stopped when he noticed that Edward had already pressed the same button.

"Seems we're going to the same floor," the older man spoke.

Edward acknowledged his comment with a smile.

"Smells good." The old man leaned closer to the apple pie and for a frightful second Edward thought the man might reach out a finger to sample it. "My wife used to cook 'em like that." Edward did not comment, so the old man held his own one-sided conversation. "Yep. She sure could cook. That woman could soothe the savage beast with one of her pies. My favorite, though, is blackberry cobbler. She'd make a blackberry cobbler that'd set your tastebuds on end. She'd serve that cobbler hot with a big ol' dollop of vanilla ice cream on top and you'd have to eat it fast 'fore the ice cream melted all down the sides."

The old man patted his stomach. "I must be hungry. Now, you take women these days—they can't cook. Want you to take 'em out to restaurants and such. My wife, she must have learned young, 'cause I married her young and from day one, she never burnt the pot."

The elevator pinged and both men stepped off. Edward moved across the hall to Kate's door while the old man hesitated, looking hard at the slip of paper in his hand. Edward rang the doorbell and waited, wishing the old man would move along down the hall.

Kate threw open the door with a smile. "Edward, I'm glad you could come on such short notice." She hesitated shyly, then stood on her toes and kissed his cheek, then looked past him.

"Harry!"

Edward stood still in the doorway, his pie going unacknowledged as Kate moved past him to wrap her arms around the older man.

"I was starting to worry about you. Did you have trouble with traffic?" Then turning back to Edward, she touched his arm. "Edward, this is Harry and Harry, this is Edward, whom I've told you about."

Edward was taken back. He had just ridden down on the elevator with Kate's husband and had been unaware of it. Was it really possible she could have married someone so much older?

"So, this is your friend." Harry made no effort to shake hands, but Edward had to admit that it would have been difficult with a pie in his right hand.

Kate looked down at the pie. "Oh, come in and put that down." It was still too warm for her to relieve him of it. "You didn't have to bring anything."

She gestured toward the kitchen and Edward went in while Kate turned back to welcome in Harry. Edward strained his ears to hear what Kate whispered to him.

"I'm warning you, Harry. Be nice."

"I was all kinds of nice on the elevator. He just ain't much of a conversationalist."

The oven door stood open and Edward looked inside. Kate had already baked a blackberry cobbler. Edward set the pie on the edge of the stove with a clatter. He suddenly felt stupid for his efforts.

Outside, Kate brushed a piece of lint from Harry's sleeve. She offered to take his coat, but he refused. "Nah, I've gotta go back down for my bag. I just wanted to make sure I could find your apartment again." He turned and left before Edward was out of the kitchen.

"Edward, sorry to spring Harry on you like this. I wanted to warn you ahead of time and I had hoped you would get here before Harry. I hope you don't mind having dinner with the two of us.''

Edward shook himself from his stupor. ''Not at all. He seemed a very amiable fellow in the elevator. I only hope that now that he knows who I am he won't think less of me for not holding up my end of the conversation.''

Kate smiled. ''I can well imagine that Harry didn't give you a lot of opportunity to talk. Once you get him going he's hard to stop.''

Edward paced across her empty living room. ''I have to admit though, I'm surprised, Kate. I didn't think Harry knew where you lived.''

''He hasn't been here above a half dozen times. He hates traveling. In fact, I was shocked when he said he was going to spend the night. We never went on lengthy trips before because he wants to sleep in his own bed every night. When he said he could stay the weekend though, I was floored.''

''The weekend!? You're going to let him stay here?''

Kate smiled. ''I know. It's a bit Spartan, but we'll survive.''

Edward paced back toward the kitchen, pausing to glance through the doorway to Kate's bedroom. Nothing had changed. Her smallish double mattress was centered under the two windows. He looked back to the empty living room. Kate had not added any furniture to her apartment since the last time he had visited. There were no other visible sleeping accommodations. He shook his head and ran his hand through his hair, making it stand on end.

''But after the reasons he gave you to leave him in the first place . . . I mean . . .'' Edward ran his hand through his hair again. ''I guess I'm just old-fashioned. I can't see it.''

Kate scowled. ''It's not like I'm moving back in with him, Edward. It's just a weekend. I can handle Harry for a weekend.''

Edward shook his head and followed Kate who had disappeared into the kitchen.

''By the way, thanks for the pie.'' She looked over her shoulder as she pulled the cobbler out of the oven and set it on the stove next to his pie. ''That was really very sweet of you. You didn't have to.''

"I'm sorry to duplicate your dessert efforts."

Kate leaned back against the counter, but glanced over her shoulder at the blackberry cobbler. "It's Harry's favorite. He would expect it."

"He mentioned it in the elevator. He said you were a very good cook."

"Well, I don't know about that. I learned a few of his favorites. What's your favorite?"

She took a step closer and Edward moved an imperceptible inch away. "Dessert or main course?"

Kate took another step closer and leaned her hip against the countertop. She faced him and he felt as if he had just been backed into a corner—which he had.

"Lasagna . . . and . . ."

Kate took another step forward.

". . . chocolate ice cream."

Their fronts almost touched. Edward put up a hand and accidentally brushed her sweater front. Startled, he pulled back just as the front door was opened.

In the next room, Harry dropped his suitcase on the floor. Embarrassed, Kate smiled, then pulled away.

"Come on," she whispered. "You can help me set the table."

The moment ended almost before it had begun and Kate turned and left him standing in the kitchen. Thankful for the support of the countertop, Edward hesitated a moment while he regained himself. Outside in the dining niche, Kate opened a closet door and pulled out what, at first, looked like a Murphy bed. It was actually a door with four short legs, no more than eighteen inches each, screwed into the four corners of the door.

Kate eased the door down onto the floor, then pulled it to the center of the dining area. She returned to the closet to produce four more large needlepoint pillows like the one in her living room. These she placed around the four sides of the table.

Finally, Edward put himself into action by moving to the closet and assisting her in the removal and draping of a large damask tablecloth. This done, he followed her back into the kitchen and waited as she handed plates to him from the cupboard.

Edward glanced at Harry as he came out of the kitchen with Kate. Harry watched him in return almost suspiciously. Edward wondered if Harry knew what they had been about in the kitchen. It did not matter. Edward cursed himself for moving in on another man's wife—even if it had not been completely of his own instigation. He reminded himself again that Kate was still married to Harry. Even if they did have an open relationship, Edward did not intend on being the third party.

"You two can sit and get acquainted while I put supper on the table."

Almost as if it took an effort, Harry moved toward the table, then slowly lowered himself to one of the pillows.

"When you gonna get some decent chairs, Katherine?"

"What's the point, Harry, if you're just gonna break them all up?"

Edward held his breath. Was Harry's destruction of her previous apartment something that they could talk about jokingly?

Kate returned from the kitchen carrying a large casserole. She placed it on the middle of the table and looked up to smile at Edward who was still standing with three plates in his hand. "Last Christmas, Harry leaned back in one of his dining room chairs and the legs snapped off of it like a couple of twigs."

"Cheap piece of furniture," Harry grumbled.

"It was over a hundred years old! But listen, Harry. I was telling Edward about that neat junk shop near you. Do you think you might be up for a visit if we rode down there one weekend? I think I may buy a couple of pieces for the apartment." Kate looked around and acknowledged her bare living conditions.

Harry shrugged and dug into the casserole before Kate and Edward had even seated themselves. "Help yourself. If you ask me, it's just sheer foolishness that you keep this place when you've got a perfectly good house." Harry looked up sharply at Edward. "I suppose Kate told you about her other place? Why she doesn't have any furniture?"

Edward felt embarrassed for the other man and merely nodded.

"Well." And he turned back to Kate. "Come on down anytime. You can stay at the house." He looked up at Edward suspiciously. "And you can stay in the carriage house."

"Harry!" Kate placed fresh rolls and butter on the table, then took her seat at one end of the low table. She blushed and glanced quickly at Edward, then diverted her attention to the casserole.

"Well, heck. I don't know how things are between the two of you. Yesterday was the first I'd heard of this young man and you said you'd known him over a month."

Kate looked toward the opposite end of the table where Edward sat. "Sorry, Edward. Harry doesn't care what he says or in front of whom." She glared at the older man to her right.

Edward felt he needed to divert any potential row, especially if Harry Delaney possessed the sort of temper that could destroy another person's home. "I'm sure Kate was absolutely honest with you about our relationship, Harry." He put down his fork and clasped his hands in front of him. "She and I are just neighbors. She's a very competent poker player and a talented artist." He smiled at Kate, then looked gravely back to Harry. "And I admire both of those qualities in her. Beyond that, I can assure you that any previous claims on her affections are sacred."

The older man snorted and took a bite of the casserole. Either Edward's assurances or the delicious casserole worked to soothe his suspicions, because he smiled. "Then I approve." Harry savored the bite in his mouth before speaking again. "You're all right, Edward. You just think of my little Katherine like that—as something sacred." He reached out to pat the back of Kate's hand.

Kate rolled her eyes and took her first bite of the casserole. Edward took a bite, but wondered how he was going to make it through the rest of the evening. The casserole, though as delicious as Harry's pronouncements, sat in Edward's stomach like a rock.

At the end of the meal, Kate brought out both desserts. Harry chose a huge helping of blackberry cobbler while Kate politely tried Edward's pie and made a great deal of fuss over it. Edward turned down both dishes and only sipped at a refill of iced tea.

Harry became almost jovial with a full stomach. He asked Edward any number of questions about owning an apartment building. Kate cut off many of his more personal questions about costs and expenses, then turned the conversation toward the renovations on Edward's apartment. Harry was happy to talk about carpentry.

When the subject turned to Kate's work, Edward mostly sat back and listened. She told about some work she would be doing at the hospital next week. She was going to be granted the opportunity to sit in on an actual operation and take photos for some study sketches. This work had nothing to do with her work for either the journal or her orthopedics project. It was a commission for a medical poster.

As the conversation turned to Harry's latest project, Kate invited everyone to take their pillow into the living room where she would serve coffee on a tray in the center of the floor.

"Nothing but nonsense, eating on the floor and sitting on pillows," Harry complained for the second time.

Edward watched as Kate picked up Harry's suitcase which he had left in the middle of the living room floor where he had dropped it. Kate carried it to her bedroom door, then without switching on the light within, merely placed it around the corner.

"I'm of a mind to make you sleep on the floor tonight, Harry."

Harry just laughed. "Did I tell you what a wonderful casserole you made, sweetie?"

Kate smiled and leaned to kiss the older man on his forehead.

Edward set his coffee cup down on the tray with a clatter. "This has been nice, but I've got to get up early tomorrow morning."

Kate straightened, "Won't you at least finish your coffee with us?"

But Edward was already moving toward the door. "It was

lovely, really, Kate, but it'll just keep me up.'' He had the doorknob in his hand.

''Well, at least let me grab your oven mitt from the kitchen.'' She rushed to the kitchen, then back to the living room. He took it from her hand, then unsure how to leave things with her in front of Harry, he tipped his head and opened the door.

''Nice to meet you, Harry.''

Kate glanced over her shoulder at Harry, then followed Edward out of the door. He was shocked when she remained in the hall, but closed the door behind her.

''I hope you haven't been put off by being thrown into an introduction to Harry without warning. He really is a very sweet old dear once you get to know him.''

Edward looked over her shoulder toward the closed door behind her. ''He seems very friendly, Kate.''

She smiled. ''He is. He's great once you get to know him.''

Edward turned and pressed the button on the elevator.

''So, good night, Edward.''

He turned back around to find Kate standing closer than would allow him to pretend he did not know that she expected a kiss. In his most brotherly manner, he bent his head and placed a quick peck on her cheek. The elevator doors opened; he stepped inside and gave a sigh of relief as the doors closed again.

Chapter Six

"Well? What'd you think?"

Harry sipped his coffee before answering. "Seemed a little jumpy if you ask me."

Kate slid the chain lock into place on the door, then moved toward the pillow where she had left her own coffee. "It was meeting you, I think. He may feel as if I've rushed him." She felt mildly depressed.

"You sure he ain't already married?"

Kate smiled sadly. "Widowed. He was married for fifteen years, but his wife died just three years ago."

Harry nodded knowingly. "That's rough. Stay that long with the same person and it's bound to be hard to start over again." His comments did nothing to improve Kate's depression. He continued. "Still, he's a young enough fellow. He shouldn't be thinking about retiring from the game just yet. You gotta be as old as me before you quit thinking about finding somebody else."

Kate scooted toward Harry and draped her arm around his shoulders. She put her head on his shoulder. "I hate to think that anyone could be too old for love."

Harry smiled and tipped his head to bump the top of hers. "Some women—like your grandma Katie—just can't be replaced or improved upon. So why try?"

They talked for another two hours before Harry finally unfolded his stiff legs and rose to go to bed.

"I've put an extra blanket on the foot of your bed and there's a night light in the plug on the right side of the mattress. Can you find everything else?" Kate was pulling the foam mattress from the front closet as she spoke.

"Don't worry about me. I can find everything I need." Harry disappeared into Kate's bedroom and she made up the mattress in the living room. It would be almost as comfortable as her own bed, but because of Harry's troublesome back she had wanted to make sure he had the support of her box springs.

Also, with Harry sleeping in her room, she would not disturb his sleep when she switched on her computer. Kate pulled the mattress closer to the wall to better reach her computer, then switched on the machine.

DaVinci has entered the room.

Kate made herself comfortable, lying on her stomach across the mattress, with the keyboard pulled under her chest.

Cyber Scribe: I was beginning to think you had abandoned me this evening.
DaVinci: Sorry about that. I've had company.
Cyber Scribe: A date?

Kate smiled. Of course he would have to pretend he did not know.

DaVinci: Two, to be precise.
Cyber Scribe: You don't mess around on a Saturday night.
DaVinci: And what about you? Did you enjoy a social Saturday night?
Cyber Scribe: I too enjoyed fine company and delicious food.

"Why, thank you, Edward." She felt a little less depressed.

DaVinci: With . . . ?
Cyber Scribe: With a lovely, yet mismatched couple.

Kate laughed out loud.

DaVinci: Sounds dull. You mean you were the spare wheel?
Cyber Scribe: Always a bridesmaid; never a bride.
DaVinci: Don't make me laugh. I'll wake up my house guest.
Cyber Scribe: Your guest is sleeping?
DaVinci: Yes, I've given up my room for the night. I'm roughing it on the floor.

There was a long pause before Edward responded again.

Cyber Scribe: Sleep sounds like a wonderful idea. I think I may be able to capture some now.
DaVinci: Am I that boring?
Cyber Scribe: Not at all. Just hearing from you has made me feel better. Good night, friend.

Kate could not stop wondering what had made him lose sleep in the first place.

DaVinci: Good night, friend.

Edward switched off his computer and sat back in his desk chair. He ran his hands through his hair and felt his headache immediately diminish. So at least Kate had some good sense about the man from whom she was separated. Maybe there was hope for a future with her after all.

Harry stiffly took the two steps to the curb. It was not in his nature to stay indoors all day. He was used to the country air and his garden. Were he at home, instead of in the city keeping an eye on his granddaughter, he would have been in the garden an hour ago, had the earth turned and bedded for the winter, have had his coffee and eggs two hours ago, and would just now be settling into a snack of pound cake and the morning paper.

As it was, it was nearly 8:00 A.M. and he was only just

getting out to fetch his own breakfast at the diner five blocks away.

Kate was a late sleeper. She always had been, he recalled. It had been something like prying out eyeteeth to get her out of bed in the mornings. In her own home, however, Harry had gone about his morning ablutions and merely stepped around her sleeping form that partially blocked the front door. He would make the most of being in the city. He would find the company of some awake person in the diner and enjoy friendly conversation and hearty fare.

He did not have to go far. At the end of the block, he stopped. An elderly lady sat behind the wheel of her parked car, the hood up. Harry leaned into the open passenger-side window.

"You having some engine trouble, ma'am?" Having never met Vanilla Lady, he did not recognize her from Kate's descriptions.

The woman looked warily back at him. "I was, but I have a gentleman looking into it for me."

Harry craned his neck and noticed a pair of well-worn work boots sticking out from under the front of the car. "And so you do!" Harry walked around the front to look down through the engine. "You need a hand there, buddy?"

A disembodied hand was all that was visible. "Harry. Is that you?"

Harry lowered himself to his hands and knees on the pavement. "Edward. So you're handy with an automobile engine, too."

"Not very, I'm afraid. Can you give me a hand? Can you grab that alternator belt from the top while I attach it from below?"

Happy to be industrious in any capacity, Harry stood again and leaned over the grille and fished his hand past the fan to grab the top of the rubber belt Edward passed up through the engine. As quickly, Edward had his end fastened and stood up to lean over the engine beside Harry. In no time, the belt was fully attached and Edward ran the jumper cables from his own backward-parked car to Vanilla Lady's car.

"Give that a try, Mrs. Vanill—er, Gaines."

The older woman turned the key in the ignition and was rewarded with a slow start. She smiled up at him through her windshield.

Edward unattached the cables and switched off his own car, then put his hood down. "You'll want to let it run for a while to recharge your battery. And the next time you have car problems, you just give me a call before you find yourself walking everywhere."

Vanilla Lady left the sedan running while she ambled around the car to the sidewalk, pushing her walker ahead of her. "You are a dear, Mr. Tucker." She looked from Edward to Harry, this time with less suspicion of the older man's motives. "So you know my landlord? Mr. Tucker here is a real angel."

Edward rolled his eyes, then kissed the older woman on the cheek. "Be careful, Mrs. Gaines." Then turning to Harry, he said, "So, you're up bright and early today. Have you had breakfast?"

Harry grinned. "You know my mind."

"Just feeling a hunger pang myself." Edward turned and led the way back to the building. "You look like a steak and eggs man."

"Just what the doctor ordered," Harry agreed, patting his empty stomach.

In Edward's apartment Harry looked around admiringly, but not for the same reason Kate had the second time she had visited. It was not at all what Harry had expected and he was pleased. The thought of Kate falling for some penthouse playboy was too much. That had been the last sort she had gone for.

Edward Tucker seemed to be solidly rooted. He had a practical man's apartment. There was not a lot of furniture or bric-a-brac on the walls. Two sawhorses took up the middle of the living room floor and sawdust had been swept into a pile beside one wall.

"So, Kate tells me you're a widower." Harry did not believe in beating around the bush.

Edward looked over his shoulder, but kept walking toward the kitchen. "Yep."

"Me too."

Edward hesitated before thrusting his hands under the tap. He lathered up, rinsed, then moved to the refrigerator door. Harry came in behind him. Edward dried his hands before saying, "That's rough. How long?"

Harry leaned back on the countertop, noting the workmanship in the cabinetry. "Was married for thirty years. It was over all too soon. She passed on nearly ten years ago."

Edward removed two large steaks and the whole dozen eggs. Harry noted what a serious young man he seemed as a crease sliced his brow.

"So, you over your wife?" Harry countered.

Edward looked up from the steaks as he unwrapped them. He did not answer immediately, but motioned for Harry to follow him. They walked out onto the terrace and Edward went about turning on the gas to the grill before answering.

"I still think about her, if that's what you mean." He threw the steaks on the grill and fished for a skillet which hung on the side of the brick grill.

"Yep. Me too. It's living alone that does it, though. If I was with somebody, I wouldn't have so much free time on my hands to think. Like when Kate lived with me, sometimes days would go by without my thinking of my wife. At first I felt kind of bad about it, but now I think that was probably healthy. Living alone ain't healthy. Living alone, you never recover from a thing like that. Yep, a fellow wasn't meant to live alone. A fellow should be settled with a wife."

Edward adjusted the gas, then moved to sit at the table and motioned for Harry to join him. "I can't argue with you there."

"Yep, you marry someone and you marry for life, but it goes beyond that. It don't matter that they ain't with you every day anymore. You're still attached at the hip."

Again, Harry noted that Edward wore that serious scowl. "But certainly there are instances when married couples just have to call it quits. I thought I believed in that lifetime commitment, but certainly if you learn that it is completely one-sided, it's time to just start over."

"Well now, I can't argue you one way or the other there.

That just wasn't the case with my Katie. We were made for each other and though we sometimes had words, we never considered calling it quits. Words.'' Harry snorted. ''Heck, sometimes I can get down right pigheaded. Got an awful temper on me, too, but that never seemed to cause my Katie to reconsider her vows.''

Edward shook his head as if he simply did not understand the sentiment. ''You mean, you don't see it? If someone moves out, if your temper destroys their home, you don't think they're reconsidering their vows?''

Harry's eyes bugged out a little bit and he leaned into the table. ''You and your wife was separated?'' Edward had not struck him as the sort of man who had a bad temper, but maybe he had missed it.

''Er, yes, but that's not the point I was making.''

''You left her?''

''No. No, of course not. I would never have . . . I mean, I'm talking about you, Harry.''

Harry sat back and laughed. ''Me? Heck, boy. You just didn't know me and my Katie when we was together. We were one of those couples—I'd start a sentence and she'd finish it. She'd trip and I was right there to catch her.''

''And now?''

Harry gave it a great deal of thought before answering. ''I was just talking with Kate about this last night. I told her I was too old to consider change. There's no substitute for my Katie, yet, like I said, living alone ain't healthy either.''

Edward stood again and moved to the grill. He put one of the steaks into the fry pan and swished it about to make grease for the eggs, then put it back on the grill and cracked an egg into the pan.

''She's in love with you, you know.''

Edward smashed an egg on the side of the pan so hard, the shell fragmented and half of it fell into the pan with the egg.

''Phooey.'' Edward scooped the shell out, then laughed and glanced over his shoulder at Harry. ''You're imagining things.''

Harry stood up and walked around the table toward the grill. He wanted to get a better look at how it was put together. ''I ain't senile yet. I know what's right in front of my face.'' He stooped to look under the grill. A propane tank was neatly tucked under a brick niche in the back. ''It's happened before, though, you know. She fancied she was in love once before and this fellow turned out to be a real gem. Let me tell you.'' Harry ran his hand along a mortar line in the brick work. ''Fellow walked and left her high and dry. I don't intend to watch that happen again.'' Harry looked up warningly at Edward, then immediately softened. ''You do this brick work yourself?''

Harry stood up, straightening his stiff legs. Edward had forgotten the steak and eggs on the grill, so Harry pointed it out to him. ''Gonna burn the steaks, son.''

Hastily, Edward turned the steaks and dumped the eggs in the trash bin beside the grill.

Edward seemed to be thinking, so Harry gave him plenty of time. He wanted this man to be certain he was in it for a lifetime commitment before he got Kate's hopes up. Harry would not see her hurt again.

Finally, Edward put the fry pan back on the grill and confidently cracked four more eggs into it before he spoke.

''My only concern is for Kate. I don't want to see her hurt, but I don't believe it's healthy to live without risk. I wouldn't dream of interfering in another man's marriage, but I don't believe it's healthy to hang on to something that's one-sided.''

Harry was not completely satisfied with his answer, but it would have to do. He could not fault the man for being honest in his intentions. It beat making promises that he did not intend to keep.

''Then rest assured, that if you pursue Kate, I'll be keeping a close eye on you. I don't have any doubt but that Kate will follow her own heart, but if I see you're about to step on it, I'll step in.''

Their conversation afterward was commonplace, with Harry asking a hundred questions about the masonry, the grill, the terrace garden, and the greenhouse. Edward answered his questions with monosyllables and impersonal statements, but a psychic shoving match had begun with each man wearing a metaphorical chip on their shoulder.

*   *   *

Kate shifted, pulling her feet under her long nightgown, and repositioned the keyboard across her knees.

> *Cyber Scribe: But you don't doubt that their relationship is one-sided?*
>
> *DaVinci: Of course it's one-sided, but he really is the only man for her.*
>
> *Cyber Scribe: There are plenty more where he came from. She could do a lot better.*
>
> *DaVinci: He's rude and coarse and without a doubt, a bore, but in their society, it's acceptable male behavior. He is the breadwinner. She is not expected to work outside of the home. That's what she's been bred for and her only aspiration is to care for "her man."*
>
> *Cyber Scribe: Surely she can't be happy.*
>
> *DaVinci: What's not to be happy about? After all the bickering and lies, Fred buys Wilma the sabertooth tiger coat. It's poor Betty I worry about. Barney never buys her anything that Fred hasn't already purchased for Wilma.*
>
> *Cyber Scribe: Now, Betty, she's the happy one. She is Barney's soul mate. Someday Wilma will get fed up and say enough is enough. I'm worth more than a woolly mammoth garbage disposal.*
>
> *DaVinci: Give me a Fred over a Barney any day of the week. At least Fred's imaginative.*
>
> *Cyber Scribe: You deserve better.*
>
> *DaVinci: Are you a Fred or a Barney?*
>
> *Cyber Scribe: Depends. Are you a Wilma or a Betty?*

Kate laughed aloud, then quickly covered her mouth, looking toward the darkened doorway to the room where Harry was sleeping. She loved when Edward flirted with her, but it would not do to read too much into it. She signed off with:

DaVinci: I'll tell you when we meet.

She was giddy and could hardly wait until the Tuesday-night poker game. It seemed like eons since she had seen Edward. She was even jealous of the morning Harry had been lucky enough to have breakfast with him.

Kate had wanted to ask Harry a thousand questions about Edward. What was he wearing? Did he smell good like he had the other night at dinner? Was he clean-shaven that early in the morning or did he wear a shadow of a beard from the day before?

Instead, Harry had only said that he could cook decent and that he was capable. He would not let the roof fall in on her head, which meant, in short, that Harry approved of him.

"Of course it will be all right. Bring Harry with you," Ned assured Kate. "Roland has had to bail on us tonight. Seems he has a cold, so we need someone else to make the numbers even."

Kate held her replenished jar of pennies level with the telephone mouthpiece and gave them a good rattle. "I've been saving my pennies again, just like you requested."

Ned laughed on the other end of the line. "Well, I just hope you saved enough, because I plan on cleaning you out again."

Just then, Kate's doorbell sounded. She knew it would be Edward arriving to pick her up, so she made her good-byes to Ned on the phone. "Thanks again, Ned. I know Harry's going to enjoy it."

Harry stepped out of the bathroom as Kate rang off with Ned. "You gonna answer the door, Katherine?"

He pulled the door open just as Edward was about to knock. "Oh. Harry." He did not cover his disappointment well. "You're still here?" Then in an effort to cover his rude question, he asked, "How are you doing?"

"I'm doing fine. Yep, I decided to stay on a couple more days. You come for Katherine?" He threw open the door to admit him, then stepped back.

"Hi, Edward. I'll be ready in just a minute." She was not used to having to share her bathroom facilities and since Harry's visit, Kate felt like she was living out of a suitcase in her own home. For someone who had very little in the way of furnishings, her apartment looked as if it had exploded.

The foam mattress with disheveled linens had been folded like a futon against one wall. Harry had insisted that, instead of calling maintenance to repair the damage done to one wall when he opened the door too sharply and sent the doorknob through the gypsum, he would do the repairs himself. Therefore another corner of the living room was taken up by a bucket of putty, a can of paint, a paint roller and handle, tray, and dropcloth. Kate tripped over the paint roller handle on her way to the bathroom. Luckily, Edward was there to catch and steady her.

"Excuse the mess, Edward. I just need to run a brush through my hair and powder my nose." She made no effort to move away from his hand which remained on her waist.

Edward looked around the room and his expression was one of surprise.

"You know, Kate, I didn't call you first. If you and Harry have plans for this evening I'm sure Ned will understand."

"No problem," she called from the bathroom. "I just got off the phone with Ned and he's looking forward to meeting Harry." She popped her head back around the door frame. "Roland's out sick, so Harry will be making the numbers even. I hope you won't mind giving us both a lift."

Edward hesitated before answering—not long enough for anyone but Kate to notice—then sounded cordial. "Of course not," Kate heard him speak to Harry in the next room while she proceeded to brush her hair. "I'm glad you could fill in."

"Haven't had me a good ol' game of poker in a while. Should be fun," Harry enthused.

Kate rummaged the bathroom vanity for the bottle of vanilla extract, then dabbed some on her neck and for good measure put another couple of dots on each wrist.

"This is a pretty big building. You handle all of the repairs yourself?" Harry asked.

"Heavens no. The management company handles that sort of thing, although I'm available if you ever need help. Kate," he called to her from the living room, "you seem to have quite a project going on here."

"They don't build 'em like they used to," Harry complained as he thumped the damaged wall with his fist. "I flung the door open the other night and put the doorknob right through the wall."

Edward looked up at Kate as she returned from the bathroom. His expression displayed something like alarm. "Was . . . anyone hurt?"

Kate was just pulling on a brown velvet blazer over brown denim pants and off-white jersey turtleneck. "Heavens no. It was just a doorknob." She sank an earring through one lobe, then began putting on the second. "Well, I'm ready if everyone else is."

Edward stepped back to hold the door for Kate and Harry, then obliged them by locking the door behind him. The elevator had arrived by the time he had joined them across the hall and they all stepped on.

Kate fished in her handbag for her necklace and thought about the last time she had been going down on the elevator with Edward. He had fastened her necklace for her. It only seemed right that she should hand her necklace to him again, then turn and lift her hair for him to fasten it for her.

Edward hesitated, then handed the necklace across her shoulder to Harry. "I can't see very well in this light. Perhaps Harry could do this for you."

Kate turned. Edward avoided eye contact and they rode the rest of the way down on the elevator in silence, Harry fastening her necklace for her.

Thirty minutes later, Edward pulled his car along the curb on a street lined with brownstones. Kate sat in the front with Edward while Harry had volunteered to sit in the rear. She kept glancing at the side of Edward's face as they talked.

"I believe Kate mentioned that you live on a farm?"

Harry sat forward in his seat, leaning his elbows across the backs of the two bucket seats in front of him. "We have a couple hundred acres. It's small by the standards of those big corporate farms nowadays. Seems everything's gone big business."

"We?" Edward questioned.

"Huh?"

"You said 'we.' 'We' have a couple hundred acres."

"Oh," Harry caught on. "We. Me and Katherine. It seems all farms these days have gone corporate."

They were out of the car and walking toward a brownstone a few houses away from where they had parked. The whole while, Kate tried to figure out what she had done wrong. Edward was being decidedly cold to her. He had barely spared her a glance since he had arrived, and what was the whole deal with her necklace on the elevator? For practically the entire drive he had carried on a conversation with Harry through the rearview mirror, barely sparing her a nod.

Almost as soon as her thoughts materialized, Kate felt guilty. Was she already getting possessive? The last thing she wanted to do was to get too clingy. Besides, there were still his feelings for Claire Cavanaugh to be dealt with.

Edward pressed the doorbell.

Ned was pulling the door open almost before Edward had released the bell.

"Come in. Come in." He limped backward to admit his guests.

"Hey, no crutches?" Edward noticed almost immediately.

"Got rid of the darn things two days ago. I'm practically skipping now."

Claire was also just inside the door. Edward had stepped back to admit Kate and Harry before him, so Kate was the recipient of a friendly kiss on the cheek from Ned, then a warm embrace and kiss from Claire.

"Ah, I forgot my pennies in the car," Kate remembered.

"No problem." Edward turned and left the crowded foyer to retrieve them for her.

Kate turned back around to the small gathering in the foyer. "Claire, Ned, allow me to introduce you to my grandfather, Harry." She took Harry's elbow. "Harry? Please meet Claire Cavanaugh and our host for the evening, Ned Mackey."

Harry hastily wiped the palm of his hand on the side of his pants, then extended it to take Claire's hand. "Pleased to make your acquaintance."

"Likewise." She smiled sweetly.

Harry was slow in taking Ned's proffered hand, but only

because he had not released Claire's hand in a timely fashion. "Ned. Thanks for letting me tag along this evening."

"Glad to have you. I feel as if Kate is already family and we're glad to meet one of her kin."

Edward was just returning as Ned said this. He glanced from Kate to Harry, then back to Kate as he handed her the jar of pennies she had forgotten on the floor of the car.

"Well, everybody get inside. It's starting to get cold out." Ned gestured for everyone to follow. Kate lingered in the foyer, allowing Harry to tag along behind Claire.

"Are you all right, Edward?" Kate put a hand on his sleeve to prevent him from following the party into the room where Ned had led them.

"Of course. Is there any reason I shouldn't be?"

"I don't know." She released his sleeve. "I just thought . . . you've seemed reticent since you came to pick me up. Are you disappointed that Harry came?"

Edward shook his head, but said unconvincingly, "No, of course not."

"I'm sorry, Edward. It was you I should have first telephoned to see if it would be all right for Harry to join us. I just didn't think."

"No, really, Kate. I'm happy to see you and Harry together."

Kate scowled. "Then is it something I've said or done?"

Edward had seemed half-distracted, looking through the arched doorway at Harry, Claire, and Ned as they made themselves comfortable in the oak-paneled living room. He turned his full attention back to Kate at her question.

"Why no. Of course not, Kate." He sighed deeply. "I'm sorry if I've given you the impression that I was upset with you. I'm really not."

She put her hand back on his sleeve to keep him from moving away from her. "Then you're not feeling well?"

Now Edward smiled down at her and gently patted her hand on his sleeve. "I feel fine, Kate. I apologize if I've been neglecting you. It's just that . . . I don't want to offend Harry by doing anything for you that he may think of as his duty."

Kate smiled with relief. "Oh, is that all?" She stood on her tiptoes and gently planted a kiss on Edward's cheek. "If it's any consolation, Harry has given you his seal of approval."

"Well, y'all coming in?" Clarence, who had emerged from the kitchen to join the group in the living room, called to Edward and Kate.

Shyly, Kate broke away from Edward with a smile, then preceded him into the living room.

Edward followed Kate into the living room, but broke away from the group to corner Clarence.

"Clarence," he whispered. "I missed Kate's introduction of Harry when we came in. How'd she introduce him?"

Clarence looked at Edward over his half-moon glasses which he perpetually wore low on the bridge of his nose. "Standing on her head, of course."

"What?"

"What are you talking about?"

Edward sighed with exasperation. "How did she introduce him so that everybody immediately thought of him as her 'kin'? Did she say, 'this is my husband,' or 'I'd like you to meet my estranged, soon-to-be ex-husband?'"

Clarence shook his head with that "you're crazy" look.

"And don't look at me like that."

Clarence pursed his lips, then said, "I wouldn't know. I was in the kitchen when she made her introductions."

"Darn." Edward snapped his fingers. "Claire," he thought aloud and began moving toward her. Harry was holding a chair for her at the wooden game table in the center of the living room floor.

"You sit right here beside me, Harry," Claire was inviting.

Edward stopped halfway across the room and stood beside Kate. He couldn't very well ask Claire how Kate had introduced Harry if Harry was sitting right beside her. He glanced at Kate and realized she was intently watching Harry and Claire. He looked back to the couple and saw them as Kate must be seeing them—like a couple. He never would have suspected it of Harry, but Kate had said that their initial separation was due to his infidelity. His brotherly defenses kicked in and he moved away from Kate and took the seat on the other side of Claire.

* * *

"I'll see your nickel and raise you two cents."

The stakes were getting high and Ned fidgeted. It was neither a sign of a good nor a bad hand. He was just tight with his pennies.

"I fold." Edward laid his hand facedown on the table and rose from his chair. He walked toward the kitchen to refill his glass of ice water.

"That's seven cents and I'll raise another penny," Claire countered.

Harry smiled, but folded. He had a winning hand, but as he was a guest, he was too polite to clean out his host.

"I fold."

"Fold." Kate and Clarence followed.

Ned called Claire out by tossing in his last three cents. "Let's see what you've got, baby cakes."

Claire rolled her eyes, then flipped her cards over to reveal a pair of fours.

Ned laughed and began raking in the sizable pile of pennies.

"Wait. Let's see what you've got," Claire demanded.

Ned flipped his cards over with his one free hand. He carried a pair of fives and a pair of nines.

Claire just shrugged and rose from her chair. She had come out the winner in the end anyway. Her reserve pennies overflowed from the bag she had brought them in. "I just thought it would be rude of me to leave the table winning."

"You're not planning on leaving?!" Ned was already shuffling the deck for the next hand.

"It's after midnight!" She moaned.

"The evening's young," Ned complained, but everyone seemed to be calling it quits. Chairs were pushed away from the table and glasses, cups, and saucers were being cleared away.

"I've taken your pennies and now I intend to steal a paper cup from your kitchen in order to cart home my winnings," Claire teased and moved toward the kitchen.

Harry was quick to follow Claire, but behind him he could hear Kate attempting to console Ned.

"How about my place next week? You could take back

those pennies you lost from Claire and line your pockets with a few more of mine.''

Ned raked his few pennies from the side of the table into his hand, then pocketed them. ''Guess that'll have to do.'' Then louder, so those in the kitchen could hear, he said ''Poker at Kate's place next week! Bring your pennies and fear in your veins.''

Harry smiled. These were a nice group of people. If the company he kept was any reflection on him, this Edward fellow might not be all bad. In particular, Edward's friend, Claire, was stunning.

She had a classic beauty about her. She was polished, just like the big city she lived in. She was trim, neat, tall, wore her hair up just so, and smelled like some kind of fancy perfumed department store. She was a working woman, too, like his granddaughter.

At first, he had not thought much of Kate's going to college to study art, but it seemed it had lots of practical applications. Kate could draw like a wonder and teach doctors how to operate. Claire, he had learned through the course of the evening's conversation, had also studied art and she decorated people's homes.

Once he might not have thought of that as a practical sort of thing to study, but he reconsidered as he listened to her talk about her work. He imagined that she helped people like Kate who did not have the time or inclination to buy their own furniture.

He wanted to see this young woman in action and he contrived a means of doing so. Cornering her in the kitchen, he broached the subject.

''So, you interior decorators, you help people pick out furniture that will suit their taste?''

''Sometimes.'' Claire reached past Edward who was blocking her way into the cupboard and pulled out a paper cup. ''Some of my clients want an entire house decorated while others may only want help in selecting a wallpaper that will match their throw pillows. My latest project has been a country bed-and-breakfast. It's my job to fill the room with comfortable, durable furniture that also will make a guest feel right at home.''

"So you could help someone pick out a piece of furniture that was going to be a gift for someone else?''

Claire nodded and smiled sweetly.

"Then I was wondering if I could hire your services.'' Then in a conspiratorial tone, Harry looked over his shoulder quickly before continuing, "I want to get a decent desk and chair for Kate. It's gotta be something she can put her computer on, but it should also be something she can work at when she does her painting.''

Claire leaned back against the counter and looked surprised.

"That's a very personal piece of furniture you want to purchase. Are you sure you don't want to consult with Kate first?''

But Harry was already shaking his head. "Oh no. It's gotta be hush-hush. If she thinks I'm gonna be spending a lot on her she won't want me to do it, but if it's already done and something that can't be returned, then there's no point in her saying, 'Oh, Harry, you shouldn't have.' I already will have and she'll have to accept it.''

Claire laughed, already enjoying the impending surprise.

"Harry? Edward? Are you two ready to pack it in for the evening?'' Kate's entrance resulted in three guilty heads turned in her direction.

"Sorry, Kate. I've been monopolizing your men,'' Claire joked, then hastily grabbed a small notepad from Ned's refrigerator front and jotted something there.

"Harry, I've enjoyed chatting with you this evening.'' With a flourish, she ripped off the top sheet and handed it to him. "This is my phone number. If you're going to be in the city for a while give me a call sometime.''

Harry smiled and felt an odd stirring in his stomach he had not felt in a long time. He checked himself. Claire was only helping him to keep his surprise for Kate a secret. "Thank you, ma'am. While I'm still in town I'd like that very much.'' And he resolved to give her a call first thing in the morning.

Chapter Seven

Just what exactly was Harry plotting by buying Kate expensive gifts? Edward found himself unable to keep up his end of the conversation on the drive home, but neither Kate nor Harry seemed much inclined toward conversation. Edward could not help but suppose that Kate was upset about all of the attention Harry paid to Claire and Claire's blatant invitation to Harry. What could Claire have been thinking? He was only barely able to concentrate on his driving and Edward was glad when he saw their building come into sight.

"I can drop the two of you off at the door before I park."

"Nonsense," Kate declined, then turning to look over her shoulder, "Harry, you can go on up. You've got the key. I'll ride with Edward then walk him back—protect him from muggers."

Harry leaned forward as Edward pulled the car up to the curb and slapped him on the shoulder. "Tucker, it was fun. Had a fine time with your friends. Nice group of people."

"Glad you could join us."

Harry was out of the car almost even before the words were out of Edward's mouth, but he did not pull away from the curb immediately. Instead, he turned in his seat to face Kate.

"Are you sure you shouldn't walk him upstairs? I can park the car myself."

"I'm sure you can." She also turned in her seat and smiled up at Edward. "But I'll enjoy the walk and I'm not ready to be shut in for the night yet."

He hesitated a moment before turning back to face the

wheel, then put the car into drive and pulled away from the loading zone curb.

"Thanks, Edward. I had fun tonight. I hope you enjoyed yourself this evening."

"Did you really? Have fun, I mean?"

"Yes. I said I did." She looked at him quizzically.

They rounded the corner at the end of the block and Edward put on his signal to wait for a car that was just pulling out of a space.

"I just thought . . . you don't mind that Claire as much as asked Harry out on a date?"

Kate scowled. "I'm only confused by his acceptance." She quickly reached over to touch his sleeve. "I mean, I'm not surprised that he should find Claire attractive. She is very beautiful. It's just that Harry has always been so adamant that he had retired from that sort of game. In fact, just the other night we were talking and he said he was content to keep things status quo."

Edward was not confused. Once a philanderer always a philanderer, he supposed. He did not voice his thoughts. "He said about the same thing to me the other morning when we had breakfast together."

Kate smiled again. "I'm so glad the two of you seem to have hit it off. He really does like you."

"But he *loves* you." Edward's tone was serious. He opened his door and moved around the front of the car.

Kate's smile broadened and she gave him her hand as he opened her door for her. Edward stiffened a bit when she tucked her hand in the crook of his arm, but in the end it just felt right. He put his other hand over hers and they walked slowly around the corner.

"You weren't upset that he paid some attention to Claire?"

But Kate was already shaking her head. "I love Harry. I want nothing more than for him to be happy." She hesitated before continuing. "I was afraid, however, of what you'd think about it."

Edward stopped walking and dropped her arm. "I'll be perfectly honest with you, Kate. I'm just a little put back by it all. I'm confused about your complacency and while ordinarily, the age difference between Harry and Claire might have given me pause, obviously that's not an issue with you." Distracted, Edward moved toward the bus stop bench and sat down on it, his back to Kate. "Call me old-fashioned, but I believe in marriage and it's hard for me to think it's right to play the field even if you are separated. That marriage has to be given a fighting chance."

"That's the pot calling the kettle black." Kate said it under her breath, but Edward heard her and turned in his seat to look up at her. "Because of my own separation?"

Kate moved around the bench and sat down beside him. "I don't know much at all about your own separation. You haven't said much about it." She hesitated before asking, "Weren't you happy in your marriage?"

Edward shrugged his shoulders. "At first I was. It was the order things were supposed to happen. We were supposed to go to our high-school prom together, then college, then marriage. I suppose we were on the youngish side when we married. I was always working. In fact, to this day, I don't really know what my wife did with her spare time. Eventually it became obvious that we were building different interests. I neglected her and she found someone else with similar tastes who filled her days. Her announcement that she was leaving me hit me hard, but more from the surprise. I was the professionally adventurous one, but she was socially adventurous. I was bowled over by her seemingly sudden decision and I felt cheated and left behind. However, in looking back, I can well see that she was the one who had been cheated for years." He sighed deeply.

Kate nodded understandingly. "And that's why you haven't made your move yet." She paused thoughtfully. "I guess Claire and Clarence are both good friends?"

Edward thought she was changing the subject. "Yes. I've known them both for years. Clarence was great to me when my wife left."

"And now you're being a good friend to Clarence."

They fell silent for a short span before Kate added, "I just think, if Claire and Harry see no impediment in their own minds, then they're free to find comfort in each other." She swallowed hard as if the next words were difficult to get out. "Maybe Harry will be a transition person and if someone else were to come along afterward they might stand a chance." She laughed unconvincingly. "They're just going on a date."

"Of course, Kate. There's still a chance." And he patted her hand consolingly. "And what about me? Do I stand even a ghost of a chance?"

Kate smiled wanly up at him. "Of course you do." She did not sound convincing. "All you have to do is act on your feelings. I hope I haven't said anything that made you hesitate before. I suppose once someone has decided their marriage is over there's no point in waiting for the paperwork to come through. It looks as if Harry may have beaten your time, but you can still catch up."

Edward looked down at his hand in his lap. It wasn't the sort of encouragement he had hoped for, but it was better than nothing. Harry might have "beaten his time," as Kate put it, but what was their relationship built on anyway? Harry had just been in the right place at the right time, offering Kate comfort and a home when she was very young, after her parents had died. Harry was, at best, an opportunist. Surely he had had his share of second chances with Kate.

"Will you go out on a date with me? I mean, not just to someone's house to play poker, but a date. Dinner? Dancing? Or maybe a movie?"

Kate reached over and took his hand. "That all depends. Are you just asking me out to make somebody else jealous?"

Edward held her gaze and squeezed her hand. "Most definitely not. Let Harry and Claire find their own happiness. I *know* what would make *me* happy."

Edward slowly leaned forward, all the while watching her face to gain a hint of her reticence to proceed. She only looked up at him, so he continued until their lips met. All the while, he waited for her to pull away, but she did not and only intensified their kiss. He felt something stirring inside himself that he hadn't felt in ages. Unwillingly, it was he who finally pulled away from her.

"I'd better get you home before you're missed."

Kate nodded. "I'll be so glad when I have my place to myself again."

Edward wondered why she did not just ask Harry to leave if his visit was unpleasant.

They rose and Edward tucked her hand back in the crook of his arm, covering her fingertips with his other hand. It was early November and getting cold—too cold to have lengthy conversations on a bus stop bench at 1:00 A.M.

Inside the building, they rode up on the elevator together. The doors opened on Kate's floor and this time, almost shyly, she leaned forward and planted a kiss on his cheek.

"Friday evening? Do you think you could get away?"

Kate nodded then stepped off the elevator. She did not speak. The doors closed between them and she was gone.

Kate wondered if there were things that Edward would talk about with DaVinci that he would not share with her personally. Mostly she wondered if Edward knew about the lunch date Harry had had with Claire just a few short hours ago.

DaVinci: So how are things going between you and the married woman?
Cyber Scribe: This is a sore subject with me just now.
DaVinci: Sorry. I didn't mean to pry.
Cyber Scribe: No. Not at all. Maybe it would do me good to get the female perspective on a few nagging points.
DaVinci: Fire away.
Cyber Scribe: Well, she had finally agreed to see me . . .

Kate felt something like a knife in her heart.

. . . but it may be because her husband has been seeing someone else.

Poor Claire, Kate thought. How could Clarence do that to her?

*I'm only afraid she may be using me to get her hus-
band's attention. At the same time, I feel more than a
little guilty about not caring. I'll accept her attention
any way I can get it.*
DaVinci: *Sounds like you're not giving yourself enough
credit.*
Cyber Scribe: *As unhealthy as it might be, I think I'm
beyond the point of caring about the potential, inevitable hurt. There comes a point in a relationship when
you have to commit no matter what the consequences.*
DaVinci: *So when are you seeing her?*

Kate only wanted to know whether their date was before or
after his date with Claire. She hoped she would be seeing him
after. She wanted to have an opportunity to erase Claire from
his memory. His response was slow in coming.

Cyber Scribe: Friday.

"Friday!" she cried aloud, then because Harry was tinker-
ing with some cabinetry in the kitchen, she said silently to
herself, "I guess you can't have a very long date if you're
picking me up at eight." She wondered if he would kiss Claire
the way they had kissed last night. To Cyber Scribe she only
said:

DaVinci: *Good luck.*
Cyber Scribe: *Thanks. I'll need it. How are things with
you and the kook?*
DaVinci: *Swimmingly. He's beating your time. Jealous?*
Cyber Scribe: *Green.*
DaVinci: *Don't worry. I'm waiting for you. I can't wait
until we meet.*
Cyber Scribe: *You'll hate me when we do. You'll prob-
ably never want to speak to me again.*
DaVinci: *My best friend? No way. And besides, it's you
who will probably never want to speak to me again.*

* * *

Edward pushed his hands through his hair, making it stand on end. He worried that he might have said too much about his date with "the married woman" on Friday night. Kate might start putting two and two together and figure out that he was Cyber Scribe.

He called to Clarence in the outer office as he walked toward his desk. "Hey, Clarence?"

Clarence could be heard pecking at his keyboard with two fingers. "Yep?"

"I didn't get a chance to talk to you last night after the game broke up. So, what'd you think of Harry?"

Clarence stopped typing long enough to look up at Edward. "I wouldn't have believed it if I hadn't seen it with my own eyes. He's old enough to be her daddy. Heck, he could be her granddaddy. Makes me feel like there might yet be hope for me."

"Kate and I talked last night. We're going out on Friday."

Clarence looked over his glasses with his disappointed-father look. "Tucker, I thought you weren't gonna pursue it."

"Maybe the talk you should be having is with your sister. I don't think she understands what's going on between Kate and Harry." Clarence only looked at him blankly, so Edward explained. "I don't know. Maybe she thought Kate was only joking about their relationship when she introduced him last night. I wasn't there, but Claire certainly didn't have the impression that they were married. Harry was conspiring to buy Kate a desk with Claire's help and when Kate walked in Claire made it look like they were just going on a date. Just a date!"

Clarence shook his head slowly. "My sister ought to know better than that. I'll have a word with her." He raised his bushy eyebrows pointedly at Edward. "And you should know better. This 'date' of yours—it's just business, right?"

"No way. It's a date."

"Wait a second." Clarence snapped his fingers, then fished through the top drawer of his desk, pulling out Edward's calendar and running his finger down the page until he came to the note that had jostled a memory. "Yep. You can't be up to no good with that girl. You've got a business dinner Friday

night." He snapped the book shut. "So there. You just call
that little married lady back up and cancel."

"Let me see that," Edward demanded, and held out his
hand. Clarence passed him the appointment book which Edward scanned, then swore under his breath.

Edward picked up the phone on Clarence's desk. He hoped
Kate would be off-line by now and have her phone line open.
He dialed the number which he had memorized weeks ago,
then waited as it rang. Clarence got up and made the pretense
of filing something, but could easily be heard muttering.
"That'll serve you right—stepping in on another man's wife."

Edward rolled his eyes, then straightened when Kate answered the phone.

"Hello?"

"Hello, Kate. It's Edward."

"Edward!"

In the background, Edward heard what sounded like a thousand glasses smashing, then Harry's oath.

"Kate. Are you all right?"

"Edward, hold just a minute, will you?" She dropped the
phone, then could be heard running through her apartment.
The next thing Edward heard was Kate's scream of pain.

"Kate. Kate. Are you all right?" Edward called into the
phone, feeling suddenly helpless. He was about to hang up
and dash out the door when the receiver was picked up again.
"Kate?" But whoever picked up the receiver merely slammed
it back onto its cradle and the line went dead.

Edward was halfway down the hall before he realized his
keys were in his desk drawer. He ran back through the office,
sparing an alarmed Clarence the briefest explanation.

"It's Kate. I think Harry may be tearing up her apartment
or something. I've gotta run."

"Don't get yourself mixed up in this, Tucker." But Clarence's words were wasted on Edward. He ran out into the hall
again, and unable to wait for the elevator, he took the stairs
two and three at a time to the parking garage in the basement.

He felt no qualms about parking his car half on the curb,
half in the street in the loading zone in front of the apartment

building. In the lobby he pressed the elevator button three times in quick succession.

His stomach lurched as the elevator doors opened on the sixteenth floor to reveal Kate's door standing open. Her cat sat in front of the open door as sentry—too wary to explore farther, curious about the new terrain. Without knocking or announcing himself, Edward pushed past the door and hastily looked about the living room. The apartment seemed deserted and no more a mess than the other night when he had come to pick up Kate and Harry. In fact, it was more tidy.

Her living room was vacant of the mattress and linens that had cluttered it before. Her computer and the large needlepoint pillow were the only evidence that someone lived there.

"Kate?" he called.

There was no response, so he more slowly walked toward the kitchen. It was there that he froze and visibly paled.

The shelf that used to hold Kate's glassware lay on the floor and the glassware that had been on it lay smashed all around. This alone would not have caused him too much alarm, but the blood did. A large bloody handprint, obviously Harry's, was on the wall above where the cabinet used to be. More alarming, however, was the small puddle and the trail of blood that dripped all the way out of the kitchen. A previously white-and-blue-checked tea towel lay on the counter, most of it covered in blood.

Edward turned around sharply and ran to the bathroom. "Kate! Are you here?"

Again, there was no response, but he found another trail of blood droplets, some of which had been stepped in by Harry's work boots and tracked out of the room again.

Finally, Edward noticed the almost indiscernible trail of blood that crossed the living room carpet and ended at the closet. Hastily, Edward jerked the closet door open, not knowing what he might find.

The mattress and a neatly stacked pile of linens was all that was hidden there. Both Kate's and Harry's coats were gone.

So this was why Kate had not asked that Harry leave her home earlier. He had a violent temper and Kate must have been afraid to ask him to leave. Of course, if he had destroyed her home once before, he would not be beyond destroying it a second time.

Edward blamed himself as he dashed back out the door, pushing the cat back inside before closing the door behind him. He should have seen the signs, he berated himself as he pressed the elevator button several times although it had not moved from the sixteenth floor and took only as long as it took the doors to open at their usual speed. He felt he had not made it clear enough to Kate that she could always turn to him for help.

He wondered if he should have just told her early on in their relationship that he was Cyber Scribe. She always referred to him as a friend when they were on-line and maybe she could have trusted him enough to seek his help. Edward remembered Harry's bloody handprint on the wall and wondered if Harry had ever hit Kate. Physical violence was definitely a possibility with someone with a temper as volatile as Harry's seemed to be.

Back in his car, Edward sped toward the hospital. Most of the drive he would later remember as a blur. He remembered running several red lights with his hazard lights flashing and his horn blaring, but in less time than it might ordinarily have taken him to drive to his office which was half the distance, he pulled into the hospital parking garage and ran the full block to the emergency room entrance.

He charged up to the admittance desk.

"Kate. Kate Delaney. Do you have her here?"

The attendant behind the desk seemed to be quite used to being thus accosted and only scanned the screen on the monitor in front of her.

"Someone just came in with that last name, but it wasn't a woman. We have a Harry—" she was explaining when Kate tapped Edward on the shoulder from behind.

"Edward? Are you all right?"

Edward spun around, and wrapping his arms around her, he held her tight until she could hardly breathe.

Excepting the seriousness for her reason for standing in a hospital emergency room, Kate could not help but laugh as she finally pushed herself out of Edward's clench with a gasp for air.

"He's fine, Edward. Really. Well, not exactly or we wouldn't be here, but the doctor seems to believe it'll just require a few stitches once they stop the bleeding."

She looked up at him with a smile. "Harry has what the medical staff around here refer to as a 'bagel injury.' "

Finally, Edward looked down at Kate. The front of her white turtleneck shirt was covered in blood. He reached out and grasped the tail of her shirt, still standing very close to her.

"I thought—I saw the blood in your apartment—and when you rang off so hastily, I was certain something had happened to you."

"Oh, Edward." She hugged him around his middle again. "I am so sorry. I should have explained. I just never thought you'd go to the apartment and see the mess I know we must have left there. I should have phoned you as soon as they admitted Harry."

But Edward was shaking his head. "Kate, how can you go on like this? This could have been very serious." He seemed almost angry.

Kate looked up with a puzzled expression. "I'm sorry, Edward. I don't think we caused any permanent damage to the apartment."

"And you know very well I'm not talking about the apartment." he flared at her. "Domestic disputes have a way of continuing unless the circle is broken, and each time they become more and more violent."

Kate's expression lightened. "Domestic disputes? Edward, what are you talking about?" She sighed and took her arms from around his middle, then taking his hand, led Edward to the seats in the waiting area. "It wasn't any sort of domestic dispute." They sat down on a corner bench. "Harry just has an awful temper when it comes to home repairs. He saw that my kitchen shelf was on the verge of coming unattached, so he tried to pound it back in place with the butt of his hand. His hand slipped, he whacked the shelf enough to completely dislodge it, and sent his hand through several glasses before the whole thing hit the floor.'' She held up her own palm as evidence, pointing to the base of her palm where Harry had received his gash. ''The admitting doctor was afraid he might have cut through some important nerves at first, but now he believes it'll just be a matter of stitching him up, although the glass very nearly went all the way through his hand.''

Edward's expression proved that he still didn't quite believe her. Kate marveled that he could have any notion of domestic abuse in her loving relationship with her grandfather. She couldn't imagine what had given him such a ridiculous notion.

''You can go in and see him if you like. They allowed me to go back with him.'' She pointed toward a curtained-off section of the hall. ''I sat with him a while until the shock of it lessened and then I started to feel queasy.'' She looked down at her shirtfront and smiled. ''For as much gore as you may see in my drawings, I'm really extremely squeamish when it comes to the sight of blood.''

Edward looked at her unconvinced. ''But I heard you scream over the phone. I thought for sure you had been . . . are you sure none of that blood is yours?''

She laughed and looked down at her shirt again, then pulled her sweater around her middle and buttoned it to conceal most of the red-turning-brown stain. ''Believe me, if it were my blood I wouldn't be in a vertical position. Harry behaved as if it was a daily occurrence to see streams of his own blood splash on the linoleum. He grabbed a towel, then went off to the bathroom as if to stitch it up himself. He bandaged it up in such a way to prevent too much mess. He wanted to clean up the kitchen before coming to the hospital, but I shoved him into his coat and practically had to haul him out to his car.''

Edward stared vacantly at the curtained-off area of hallway. ''I guess I misjudged Harry.''

Kate laughed. ''Ah, yes.''

''So when is Harry planning on leaving?''

''He was actually going to break camp today, but now that this has happened, I don't think he should go until his hand is better. I don't imagine he'll be able to drive for a while, and then caring for himself will be a challenge.'' They fell silent for a moment before Kate broke into Edward's thoughts. "So you never did say why you called this afternoon."

Edward struggled to remember, then snapped his fingers. "Oh yeah. I almost forgot. I'm going to have to break our date for this Friday night."

Kate's stomach plummeted. "Oh?"

"Yeah. It seems I have a business dinner I forgot about, but Clarence reminded me this afternoon."

Kate only nodded numbly.

"But I hope you'll let me make it up to you. Maybe Saturday night?"

"Of course," Kate agreed, but found it difficult to hide her disappointment.

Edward did not seem to notice, however, and in a moment announced his intention to look in on Harry.

Edward felt little guilt over wanting to hear Harry's version of the story which Kate had related to him. He later told himself it was sick of him to want to hear a different version. He wanted to hear that Harry had lost his temper with Kate and was destroying her kitchen once having learned that she was on the phone with himself.

That was not to be the case, however. As Edward rounded the curtained-off bed where Harry sat upright, his elbow on a tray in front of him with his hand over his head, he knew he would not hear a different story from Harry.

"Howdy, Edward. Funny seeing you here." Harry did not sound either disappointed or overjoyed at having a visitor in the emergency room.

"When Kate rang off so hastily I went to the apartment to check on her. I saw the evidence of your accident and imagined the worst."

"Ah," Harry said understandingly. "Gave you a bit of a shake-up, did it? I told her we should've cleaned up before charging out the house. Never thought anyone would come along behind us, though." Seeming to remember his manners, Harry scooted over on the hospital bed and nodded to Edward, offering him a seat, which he declined. "So, your first thought was to check on Kate?"

Edward nodded.

"That's reassuring." Harry squinted at Edward as if he were still sizing him up. "I suppose I'll be leaving her in good hands when I head home this evening."

"You're still planning on leaving?" Edward nodded toward his hand. It was wrapped in a thick gauze treatment and a light spot of red was beginning to show through. "You think you're going to feel up to driving later?"

Harry gave his hand the briefest scrutiny before putting his elbow back on the tray and returning his hand to a position above his head. "This ain't nothing. It bled like the devil, but I barely feel it now."

Just then a nurse came into the cubicle with a metal tray. "How's it looking, Mr. Delaney?"

Harry held out his hand and lifted the gauze.

"Pretty," was her response before she rewrapped his hand with clean dressing. "Now don't keep taking the dressing off to look at it. You need to percolate a little while longer."

"Will Harry be here overnight?"

The nurse paused with the curtain pushed back in her hand. "Oh, I don't think that will be necessary, but he'll want to take it easy for a few days."

"And what about driving?" Edward continued.

The nurse shrugged. "Is there someone who could give him a lift home? I don't think he'll want to drive himself right away either."

Edward nodded and the nurse smiled at him, then left.

"Looks like you're stuck here a short while longer, Harry."

He could see determination in the older man's eyes. Harry had no intention of staying longer, and while a few hours earlier Edward would have been thrilled at the prospect of Harry moving out of Kate's apartment, now it seemed cruel to send a man his age, in his condition, away on a four-hour drive home by himself.

"But listen, if you're determined to be off I don't mind driving you home," Edward offered, feeling guilty for his ulterior motives.

Harry's eyebrows shot up. "Why, that's awfully kind of you. Awful good, but no." And in a moment he had changed the plans he seemed so set on just a moment before. "I'll hang around here another couple of days." And as an after-thought, he brightened, saying, "And you know I'm seeing that friend of yours this weekend—Claire? I was planning on driving back to the city next weekend anyway so I might just as well stick around another week." He looked up at Edward with a twinkle.

"You mean you and Claire are going out on a real date? Not just to pick out a desk for Kate? Does Kate know?"

"Well, I hadn't mentioned staying the rest of the week, but I don't think she'll mind too awful much."

"No, I mean does she know about your date with Claire?"

Harry scowled. "Come to think of it, she doesn't. I tried to tell her this afternoon when I got back from lunch with Claire, but it just didn't seem right. Seemed disloyal, if you know what I mean."

"Yes. I *do* know what you mean."

"Silly. Downright irrational of me." Harry laughed. "Kate and I have always been easy about talking with each other, but I don't know. Lately . . ." Harry looked up at Edward. "Used to be, she could tell me anything and vice versa, but seems now she's got somebody else she can confide in. Doesn't seem right it being one-sided like that."

Edward nodded. He paused, then jumped in to his next thought. "I've asked her out for Saturday night."

"Oh? I thought Kate told me Friday night."

Edward was not sure if Harry was being sarcastic. "She told you then? And you're okay with it?"

"Well I'm just as pleased as punch." Harry sobered slightly. "We are just talking about dinner and a movie, aren't we?"

Edward nodded, all seriousness. "Something like that. We haven't made any definite plans." He knew to what Harry was alluding.

"Good then. You two have fun. Maybe I'll call up Claire and see if she'd like a home-cooked meal. If you and Kate aren't going to be around I could dazzle her with my chicken and dumplings."

It had not been Edward's intention to give Harry a means

of seeing Claire in the intimate confines of Kate's apartment. "Well, you can bring that up with Kate. In the meantime, I'll just be outside in the waiting room with her."

Harry smiled. "Good. You do that. Hold her hand or something."

Edward could only shake his head as he left the curtained cubicle.

Harry nursed his bandaged hand by cradling it in his good hand. Kate was very quiet on the drive home.

"You sure you don't mind my staying another week?"

"Of course not." But her words did not seem convincing—not even to herself. "I want you to stay." She glanced his way and gave him a reassuring smile. "I see so little of you. I'm glad you're going to extend your visit. I'm just sorry it has to be because you've hurt yourself."

"I was meaning to come back to town next weekend anyway," he surprised her.

"You were?" Again, she glanced sideways at Harry before turning her attention back to the road in front of her.

"Seems I've got a date with that nice lady we met last night—Claire."

Kate scowled. "Yeah. You never did tell me about your lunch with her."

"It . . . didn't seem right," he stammered. "You're not upset, are you?"

"Why didn't you say something about it earlier?"

Harry fidgeted. "I was afraid of your reaction."

"*My* reaction?"

"I know you loved your Grandma Katie. I was afraid you'd think it was wrong of me to start thinking about seeing somebody else—especially after our talk the other night—about me not thinking about settling down with anybody else."

Kate laughed with relief. "I've told you I thought you should get out more. And it's not as if you're a recent widower. Grandma Katie's been gone for some time." On a softer note, she said, "And I think she'd be happy to know you weren't alone."

Harry was quiet a moment before speaking again. "I hope

you ain't been holding back with *your* young man on account of me. Just because you're finding happiness with somebody doesn't mean I'm getting left behind.''

Kate shook her head. ''I'm sorry if I seem hesitant, Harry.'' She glanced at him again. ''I guess I should just out with it, too.'' She took a deep breath. ''Claire is married.''

''Well, I'll be . . . Where'd you get a notion like that?''

''She's married to Clarence. They're separated, though, but that's not the half of it.''

''Any more than that and I think I'm gonna be confessing a lot at church next Sunday.''

Kate tried to smile. ''I've been holding back with Edward because I believe he's in love with Claire.''

''Phew.'' Harry shook his head and laughed. ''That's a lot of hogwash. Edward ain't head-over-heels for nobody but you.'' Reaching out his good hand, he patted her on the knee. ''And I'm pretty certain Claire ain't married.''

''What makes you think not?''

Harry shrugged. ''If she was we wouldn't never had lunch together. That's what.''

Harry seemed unconcerned about anything that Kate had told him. She only hoped he would not suffer a broken heart for all his trust. With Harry, everything was black and white. You were either married or not married. She felt certain she was setting herself up for disappointment, yet she felt unable to stop pursuing Edward. With them, nothing was black and white. It was a mottled gray.

Harry rapped on the door to the terrace apartment. He still grumbled at the idea of living in an apartment building. It just did not make sense. He simply thought, if you liked green, you ought to live in the country. Yet here was a man who obviously enjoyed a garden as much as the next fellow, yet he chose to grow his tomatoes in pots. Edward pulled open the door from the inside and ushered Harry in without preamble.

''You sure you don't mind storing this thing up here?''

Edward led the way down the hall. ''Of course not.'' He pushed open the door to his latest renovated room and stood back to admit Harry first. The new desk stood in the center of the room. Sunlight streamed in through the bank of windows along one wall and a fresh coat of paint and clear varnished floors made it seem bright even on this rainy day.

Edward stood back with his hands shoved in his pockets while Harry circled the new piece of furniture as if it might leap out and bite him. It had been delivered by two men just two short hours ago. It had taken both of the movers and Edward's efforts to secret it in his apartment.

"You think Kate's going to like it?"

With a smile, Edward confirmed, "Kate is going to love it." It was the most unusual desk Edward had ever seen and Harry gleamed with pride.

"And it don't look half bad in this room." Harry looked around the new renovation. "So what's this room going to be? Looks too big for a guest room."

Swallowing hard, Edward lied, "I haven't decided yet." He knew he had had Kate in mind the whole while he had worked on it. This room could be nothing other than an artist's studio. Originally two smaller guest rooms, Edward had knocked out one wall to make the large studio. All but one of the windows was original and he had purposefully left it unadorned. Going by her own apartment, he really had not known what else she might like in her studio.

Harry looked back to the desk. "I can't really take credit for this, though. It was Claire who picked it out."

"Claire has exceptional taste."

"Claire is a real lady." Harry watched Edward's face, trying to gauge his reaction.

Edward only nodded, then walked out of the studio. Harry followed, not at all put off by his avoidance of discussing Claire.

"Kate has some crazy notion that you're in love with her."

Stopping at the living room, he turned with a puzzled look. "In love with . . . Claire?"

Harry laughed. "There you go. It's obvious."

"What's obvious?"

"That you're not in love with Claire."

"Well, of course I'm not in love with Claire. Where'd she get a silly notion like that?"

Harry shrugged. Edward motioned toward the new sofa in the living room and Harry made himself comfortable there.

"So when you gonna make your move?"

Edward looked toward the older man with a startled expression. "I'm not sure I know what you mean."

Harry shook his head. "You young folks just don't appreciate how short our lives really are. You see something— someone—you want and you don't act. You take your time like you're some sort of dad-gum immortal. Look at me. When I met my Katie, I didn't mess around. I was in love, so I swooped her off of her feet like there weren't no tomorrow. We had a good long time together and before I knew it, it was all over and done with. It was too short." Harry snorted. "I bet I beat you to the mark again. I bet I sweep that sweet friend of yours off her feet before you've even said boo to Kate."

"You plan on sweeping Claire off of her feet?"

"I ain't messing around like you." Harry looked down at his injured hand. The bandage had been removed the previous day and all that remained of his injury was a red slash across his palm. "I think maybe my accident extended my love line."

"And what about Kate?"

Harry looked up. "Kate is happy for me."

Edward wondered. Perhaps Kate had told Harry that she thought he was in love with Claire to steer Harry away from the other woman. Maybe Kate was grasping at straws to hold on to Harry. He thought she deserved more. He wanted to give her more than the sort of helpless, loveless future that Harry would offer her. Even if Harry and Kate somehow patched things up, his philandering would always get in the way. How could she trust someone like that and have any self-respect?

In that moment, Edward made up his mind. He would not be beaten to the mark by Harry. He would turn Kate's attention away from Harry in the only way he knew how. He would stun and dazzle her with his own attentions for all the days of her life. Harry had a charming homespun philosophy which had won the heart of a very impressionable girl, but Edward had unselfish love.

Chapter Eight

Violently, Kate erased a hole through the paper on which she was drawing, swore, then tore it from her easel.

At least, she thought, Edward could pay her the courtesy of telling her the truth about his reason for canceling their date. Why should he believe that she would be upset about his having a date with Claire? Had she been wearing her feelings on her sleeve?

Instead, Kate sat home alone on a Friday night and felt gloomy. Not that this evening was any different from any other Friday night for the past year. She had never thought about her reclusive habits until now. In the past two weeks she had become accustomed to sharing her home with Harry, but she did not even have his company as he had also decided to dine out.

Kate settled into her position on the floor in front of her computer. It would feel good talking to someone—anyone on the chat group—who might lend her a sympathetic ear.

It was just as she began to power up her computer that her doorbell chimed. She glanced at the watch on her wrist. It was only a little after nine. Had Edward called his evening short with Claire? She jumped up from the floor, ran to her door, and threw it open.

"David," she greeted him with disappointment.

"Well, thanks for the warm welcome. Nice to see you, too."

"I'm sorry." She stepped back to admit her agent. "It's just that I was expecting someone else."

David wore his traditional black over black. This evening,

because it was cold out, he wore a long black coat over his dark ensemble.

"Uh-oh. Is lover boy starting to neglect you?"

Kate wished she had checked through the peephole before answering the door. She might have pretended to have been out.

"I was not expecting 'anyone'," she lied. "As it just so happens, *Edward*,"—and she emphasized his name—"is out this evening. He had a business dinner." Again she lied. After all, that was precisely what Edward had told her. There was no reason she should tell David Tipton any different.

David perused her apartment's lack of decor, sniffing with approval. He would expect Kate to have slightly eccentric taste. Kate recalled that he had never been in her apartment before, then a thought occurred to her.

"So, how'd you get into the apartment building? You need a key to get in at the lobby door."

David turned with a flourish of his long coat. "Oh, I just held the door for some little old lady with a walker. She was more than a little suspicious of me, too."

Kate could well imagine she would have been. Poor Vanilla Lady would have been too shy and polite to tell him he could not enter.

"You shouldn't prey on people's weaknesses."

"That's how I make my living." He shrugged. "I prey on people's weaknesses."

Kate was well aware of his game. Somehow it made her like him better that he would admit to it. "So what brings you over here tonight?"

David made himself at home by peeling out of his overcoat. As he looked around for someplace to hang it, Kate motioned toward the living room closet. "Thanks." He took his time hanging it up. Kate had never noticed how fastidious he was. He had always struck her as something of a clotheshorse, though.

"I just happened to be in the neighborhood. I have a date later and some time to kill beforehand, so I thought I'd pop in on you to see how things were progressing."

He walked to the large easel in the dining room, then glanced down at the torn sketch wadded up in the floor.

"So I see things are going well?" He pointed to the crumpled sketch.

Kate walked over and snatched it up, crushing it completely, then tossed it onto the kitchen floor. The cat darted out from behind the door and could be heard batting the paper wad.

David picked up another piece of work which Kate had left standing against one wall, its back to the room. It was the piece Kate had been working on as a housewarming gift for Edward. David's smile of approval was all the compliment she needed.

"So, has Harry been staying with you long?" he surprised Kate by asking.

"Well, as a matter of fact, about two weeks now. How did you know?"

David nodded toward the closet. "A man's flannel coat in the closet and an unmistakably nice car parked around the corner. You know, he really should have it garaged while he's in the city. Any number of horrible things could happen to it out there on the street."

Kate shook her head, then sat down, making herself comfortable on the pillow in the living room. "Harry's car. Is that why you've popped in? You still trying to get him to sell it to you?"

David brightened. "Is he selling it?"

"No."

"Oh." David made no effort to hide his disappointment. "So, has lover boy, er, Tucker, met Harry yet?" David slowly melted onto the floor facing Kate.

"Yes. Harry approves of him. They seem to have some common interests."

David spoke haltingly. "And does Edward approve of Harry?"

Kate's eyebrows rose. "I think Edward likes Harry fine." Kate laughed. "They've bonded over a car engine and steak and eggs."

David seemed to pale. "And Edward . . . has he told you—in certain words—what he thinks of Harry?"

Kate scowled. "Edward is very diplomatic and even if he wasn't completely awash with admiration for Harry he would be thoughtful enough to keep his opinions to himself."

She recalled Edward's words about Harry the night of the poker game. He had said that he was a little put back by Harry's behavior. He obviously thought Harry was too old for Claire, but that could be tinged by his own jealousy. Edward was a good man. Kate knew how he must be feeling about seeing Harry and Claire together. After all, she was experiencing all of the same emotions watching him pine for Claire.

David put up his hands in surrender. " 'Nuff said. I can see that this Edward wears a suit of armor in your eyes."

"Do I sound defensive?"

"You sound like you'll slay anyone who bad-mouths your man."

Kate sobered. "Well, he's not exactly my man."

"Uh-oh. There *is* trouble in paradise. Well, just tell me all about it."

For the first time in their relationship, David seemed to be genuinely concerned. Kate had not realized how badly she had needed to talk to someone, but in under fifteen minutes, she had told David Tipton about every nuance of her relationship with Edward. She hesitated before telling him about Cyber Scribe and how she had always thought of him as her best friend. That made up for the seemingly short time she had known Edward. Now, however, she did not even have him to confide in. She went into the details of Edward's deception—how he lied about having a business dinner when in fact it was a date with Claire. David was sympathetic and consoling.

"So really what we're looking at is a double affront. Not only did he stand you up, but he also lied about his reason for standing you up. You know this man is two-timing you?"

Kate laughed, but she felt far more depressed than before David had shown up on her doorstep. "That may be a bit harsh. He hasn't given me any reason to believe our relationship is exclusive."

"Then maybe you should think a little harder about what

you want from your relationships. Don't you want it to be exclusive?''

''Yes. Of course I do.''

''Then you had better find yourself a man who is willing to be exclusive—and honest.'' David threw up his hands. ''I warned you about working for this man. He doesn't have an artist's passions.''

Kate mulled over what David was saying, but almost immediately dismissed it. Of course she wanted Edward to feel free to tell her he had a date with Claire. She would rather hear the painful truth—that he chose to break a date with her in favor of a date with Claire. She hoped she understood where Edward was coming from, though, and she could wholeheartedly understand his inability to enter into an exclusive relationship with herself at this time.

As miserable as she felt, she thought she owed David something for being a sympathetic listener. Coffee and some warmed-over cobbler were his rewards. Because she felt like she needed cheering, Kate produced two candlesticks from a kitchen cupboard and, placing them in the center of the serving tray in the center of the living room floor, she lit them before settling down in front of David with a cup of coffee in her hand.

No sooner had she taken her first sip of coffee, however, than her doorbell chimed again.

''Excuse me. It's not usually this busy around here.'' Rising again, she moved toward the door, this time opening it without expectation. ''Edward!'' Her surprise and pleasure were evident.

He thrust toward her a bouquet of six pink roses wrapped in green tissue paper.

''A peace offering and humble apologies.'' Edward's gaze moved past Kate to the tray in the center of the living room floor with the candles burning on it. David Tipton was just rising from his seat and moved toward him.

Kate could practically read his thoughts and grabbed Edward's elbow to steer him into her apartment, then nodded toward her agent. ''You remember David Tipton?''

"Tipton." Edward greeted the agent with a nod of recognition.

"Tucker. Back early?" David headed toward the closet and without waiting, found his own coat and put it on with a flourish. "And just when I have to be off."

Kate smiled at her agent in appreciation for his tact. He might not have been terribly complimentary toward Edward while they were talking, but it was good of him to give Edward the benefit of the doubt and leave them alone.

"Don't leave on my account," Edward offered.

"Oh, it's not on your account," Kate explained, eager to make an excuse for having coffee with David Tipton by candlelight. "David popped in when he noticed Harry's car parked outside. He's on his way to pick up his date." Kate never closed her apartment door between Edward's arrival and David's exit.

"And I'm tactful enough to know when I'm no longer needed." David moved past Edward, stopping beside Kate. There he surprised her by leaning forward and kissing her cheek.

Kate put her hand on his arm. "Thanks for everything, David. You really are a friend."

David looked surprised, then sheepish. "Shortly I think you may have reason to reconsider that proclamation."

Kate only watched him with confusion as he looked from her to Edward with a knowing smile, then left her apartment.

"Now what do you suppose that was all about?" She looked after David as he stepped on the elevator, then slowly closed her door. She still held the flowers from Edward in her hand, and recalling herself, she smelled them appreciatively. "These really are beautiful, Edward. Let me just find something to put them in."

Edward walked to the tray in the center of the living room, and picking up the two full cups of coffee, he carried them into the kitchen behind Kate.

By now, the kitchen shelf which he had last seen lying on the floor with the shattered glassware had been reattached to the wall with new brackets and a supporting board below it. It was a crude fix, but definitely substantial. Edward left the coffee cup on the sink, then went to inspect Harry's handiwork.

"Harry insisted on repairing it even though I'm certain he shouldn't be using his hurt hand just yet." Kate searched a cupboard and finally produced a large, clean mayonnaise jar. She filled it with water, having to brush past Edward to reach the sink, then carefully arranged the roses in it.

"Has Harry suggested when he might be heading home?"

Kate found herself unable to meet Edward's gaze. Instead, she fumbled with the roses and baby's breath in the makeshift vase. "I think Harry may be staying on for a while." She drew a deep breath. "There." She put the vase of flowers away from her to inspect the arrangement. "They're beautiful." She walked back out into the living room, looked around, then decided to place them on the candlelit tray which still stood in the center of the living room floor.

Edward followed her. "And Harry—did he give you any reason why he would be extending his stay? I thought he was anxious to get home."

Again, Kate found herself unwilling to meet his gaze, but finally, she looked up at him. Edward was standing far closer than she had realized—only a couple of feet separated them. "I don't suppose there is any way around it." She watched his face for a change of expression and took a step closer. "Harry has met someone he very much admires here in the city. He is staying on so that he might see her."

Kate thought she would give almost anything to know how Edward's date with Claire had ended. The last thing she wanted to do was to hurt him if he truly believed and still hoped for a chance with Claire. "I think I should also mention, the woman he's been seeing . . . is Claire."

Edward smiled sadly. "I know."

Kate blinked. "Then she told you? Did she tell you they've seen each other almost every day this week?"

Edward's eyes widened with surprise. "No. I haven't seen Claire all week."

"You haven't?" She looked suspicious. Would he continue to lie to her?

"No. Of course I see Clarence every day, but we don't usually discuss Claire's dating habits."

"No. I don't imagine you do."

Edward ran a nervous hand through his hair. "We talk about you."

Kate looked up suddenly, then blushed. Edward was not just flattering her. He was being honest. He and Clarence really did discuss her. Edward seemed nervous and it made her a little jumpy.

"You do?" Her brain began to shut down as Edward took a step closer and with a shaky hand he ran his rough finger across her jaw. "What do you say about me?"

"I asked Clarence's advice."

Kate only looked up at him, her hand hovering between them, not quite resting on his chest, but trying to find a resting place. "Advice?"

Edward solved her predicament by taking her hand in his. "I've asked him whether or not he thought . . . it might be too soon . . . if . . ."

Kate held her breath.

". . . if I asked you to marry me."

At once, Kate felt as if her stomach had lifted like it did when the elevator came to a stop. At the same time, the blood rushed from her head and she felt swimmy.

"I . . . but you . . ." she stammered.

"Don't think, Kate. Just say yes. Say yes and we can be married . . . as soon as you're free to do so."

Kate's ears began to ring. Was she hearing him right? She looked up, searching his face for any indication that he might be teasing or joking. He could not possibly be serious—unless his evening with Claire had ended poorly.

She knew her answer, yet could she be certain that Edward would feel the same about her in the light of day? Once he had put the distance of time between himself and the rejection he must have just suffered at the hands of Claire, he would regret his hasty proposal.

Yet was it hasty? He said he had discussed her with Clarence. Perhaps that had only been a means of making Claire jealous—hoping that Clarence might report the news back to

Claire. Perhaps, probably, Clarence had told Edward about Kate's early declaration that she was going to marry him! Kate's cheeks flamed with color.

Kate reached up, touching his cheek. He had only initiated a kiss one time. The night they talked outside at the bus stop she felt certain he had been the one who began that embrace, yet once again, he had been suffering from Claire's rejection. That night Claire had flirted shamelessly with Harry and perhaps Edward had only sought comfort from Kate.

Reaching up, she touched the side of his lip. Kate took a deep breath. "In the morning, Edward. Sleep on it and in the morning, if you are still so inclined to ask, then . . . yes, I will marry you. If you change your mind between now and morning, then you don't need to say anything. I'll know."

"Eight hours won't change a thing."

Kate stood on her toes and left a feather-soft kiss on his lips. "In the morning . . ."

"I'll see you then? You'll come up for breakfast?"

Kate nodded. "I'll come up."

Edward hesitated as if he really did not want to leave her, but Kate only imagined it was because he wanted her comfort after Claire's rejection. It was painful to allow him to leave without pouncing upon his proposal, but Kate had no doubt that in the morning he would feel quite the fool for so rash a proposal.

"Cyber Scribe has entered the room."

Kate brushed the cat off of the keyboard.

DaVinci: I've been waiting for what seems like hours to talk to you.
Cyber Scribe: I need to talk to you, too.
DaVinci: Me first.
Cyber Scribe: No. Don't say anything—not until we've had a chance to meet.
DaVinci: But I'll burst!
Cyber Scribe: I'll clean up the mess.
DaVinci: Then we still have a date?

Cyber Scribe: If you're still speaking to me.
DaVinci: Why wouldn't I be speaking to you?
Cyber Scribe: I'll tell you—tomorrow.

Kate's heart pounded as she stood outside the door to Edward's apartment. What would he say to her when he opened his door?

"Well, you can't expect the man to know you're standing here. Ring the bell, Katherine."

Harry reached around her and pushed the doorbell. The sound caused her to jump. Would Edward believe she had brought Harry with her to ward off any further proposals? Was he finally going to tell her about Cyber Scribe? It had been difficult to get out of bringing her grandfather upstairs with her. He had invited himself to tag along. He was amazed that Kate had been up at an unusually early hour. When he had heard that she was going to have breakfast with Edward, Harry just seemed to assume that he too was invited and bounded along with her.

Edward threw open the door, a smile on his handsome face which faltered when he saw Harry standing slightly behind Kate.

"Good morning."

"Good morning, Edward." Kate looked up shyly, then averted her gaze.

Harry beamed from behind her, slapped Edward on the shoulder as they entered, then moved around Kate who still stood fixed in the doorway.

Edward waited, silently holding the door until Kate finally put herself into gear and stepped into the apartment.

"Excuse me barging in on you two like this," Harry spoke up. He seemed as giddy as a child at Christmas. "But when Kate said she was coming up this morning, I knew I couldn't wait until Christmas. Let's just show her now, Tucker."

Edward nodded, but still looked none too pleased. Kate chanced a glance at his face and was hopeful. Her greatest fear, one which she had wrestled with all night, was that Edward would not repeat his proposal. It seemed inevitable when Harry had announced his intent to accompany her upstairs.

''Show me what?'' she asked without really hearing what Harry was saying.

Harry was already leading the way down the hall. Kate recalled herself, then looked to her grandfather with bewilderment. When she looked back to Edward, he merely gestured for her to follow Harry.

Harry made a grand production about opening the first door along the corridor, then disappeared around the door frame before Kate had reached the spot. She stopped at the door, looking in.

Harry stood beside an ornate, antique draftsman's desk, his elbow leaning on it, but Kate took in not only the single piece of furniture, but also the newly renovated room.

''So, what do you think?'' Harry thumped the top of the oak piece, then looked to Kate for her delight.

She did not disappoint him. She circled it in silence, beaming smiles at him while she ran her hand around it. The desk stood as tall as she was with a large, sloped writing/drawing surface on one side and lower compartments on the opposite side. A door opened on the compartmentalized side to make a surface that would be suitable for storing a computer and keyboard although that had not been its original function.

Kate paused to hug the older man and kiss his weathered cheek. ''It's beautiful, Harry,'' she enthused, and kissed him a second time.

Harry blushed, then became gruff as was his habit with too-profuse appreciation. ''I'm just tired of seeing you sit on the floor to do your work. You'll get old and stiff before your time.''

Kate turned her smiling face to Edward. ''And you knew about this. For how long?''

Edward shrugged. ''It only arrived a few days ago. Harry asked if I would store it here until Christmas.'' He looked down at the date on his watch. ''Or December the tenth.''

Kate laughed and covered her mouth. This was Harry's way of saying good-bye to her. They never exchanged expensive gifts at Christmas. He knew she was in love and he wanted her to feel secure in leaving his grandfatherly care to begin a family of her own. She ran back to the older man and hugged and kissed him again, this time tears pricking at her eyes.

"Okay, okay. Enough of this foolishness." Harry kissed the top of her head, then pushed her away. "Now I'll head on down. I know you two kids didn't plan on sharing breakfast with me." Harry moved toward the door and Kate hastily brushed a tear from her cheek with the back of her hand.

On his way through the door, Harry slapped Edward on the shoulder. "You take care of her," he murmured, then disappeared. Kate turned to compose herself and looked around the room. It was obvious to her that this room was hers. It was an artist's studio and she could find some flattery in that Edward had renovated it with her in mind. He intended her to live here. The joy at being left alone to talk with Edward was mingled with sadness—both for her farewell from Harry and for the one-sided marriage Edward intended to offer her. He had material possessions to offer her, but not his heart. This sadness was reflected in her eyes.

"So you liked Harry's desk?"

She turned to face him, then nodded and averted her eyes.

"It was heavy as the dickens to move. Just from the lobby to the elevator, then into here, it took three men." Kate looked up at him without responding, so he continued. "It would be really be heavy to have to move it back down to the sixteenth floor."

"Far too much trouble," she agreed.

"It would be easier, in fact, just to move your few things up here."

Again, Kate nodded, still studying his face.

He smiled down at her, almost sadly, then turned and spoke over his shoulder. "I've made pancakes and bacon. We can eat out on the terrace."

Kate followed. She was numb inside.

Kate held her hand of cards awkwardly, conspicuously aware of the weight around her left ring finger. It was the ring which Edward had given her the morning of their breakfast together, just a few short days ago.

Somewhere between the pancakes and bacon and a refreshing melon dish to clean the palate, Edward shifted on his chair, nervously produced a small, black velvet box from his pants pocket, then slid it across the table toward Kate.

"What's this?" But she already knew and slowly, almost hesitantly, she opened it to reveal a platinum ring of diamonds mounted in an antique filigree setting.

For the second time that morning, Kate had felt tears prick at her eyes. Having recognized her emotionalism, Edward had moved around the table to her side.

"It's beautiful, Edward. I never expected . . ." But she had trailed off.

"I understand, and if you're not ready to wear it yet I'll understand that, too."

But he need not have mentioned it, for Kate had slipped the ring on her left-hand ring finger. Ordinarily, she never wore jewelry unless it was a special occasion, but this ring had fit perfectly and also had looked as if she had always worn it. She had imagined how it would look when coupled with a similar colored band.

She was used to seeing it when she awoke, yet this evening her stomach had been a jumble of nerves since Edward's friends had begun arriving at her apartment. She had hoped for an abrupt, early announcement to his friends, yet Edward had remained quiet throughout the evening. It was nearing 10:00 and still he had told no one of their engagement. She did not feel free to make the announcement herself and she worried that Edward was having second thoughts. Perhaps he had wanted to break the news of their engagement to Claire first.

"I'll see your penny," Ned countered Roland's raise in bid.

"See you." Edward threw in his two cents.

"I fold." Kate had two pair, yet she couldn't bring herself to expose her ringed hand by throwing in a bid, and discreetly covering the back of her left hand with her right, she laid her cards on the table. She excused herself from the low table in her dining area.

"I see your penny and call." Clarence closed the bids and flipped over his hand.

There was always a tumult of conversation at the close of each hand as Ned and Roland bantered over strategy and bluffing techniques. Kate stepped around the pillow on which Edward was seated beside her and made her way to the kitchen. She had made Ned's favorite "lemony things," as he referred to them, and she removed them from the refrigerator just as Clarence entered the kitchen behind her.

"You and Tucker are two peas in a pod."

Kate looked up with raised eyebrows. Clarence was helping himself to a refill of tea from the pitcher on the counter.

He filled her in. "Ain't neither one of you got two sticks of furniture to rub together to make a fire. What the two of you got against comfortable seating?" Clarence turned his question to include Edward who was just entering from the living area.

Kate smiled. "I don't know what Edward's excuse is." She sliced through the sheet pan of lemon squares, not looking at either of them as she spoke. "I lost all of my furniture to an enraged ex-fiancé. At the expense of my furniture I consider myself very fortunate to have been spared a lifetime of regret."

"Whew." Clarence whistled. "I'd say so. You mean this fellow, whoever he was, tore up your furniture? Was he taken to drink?"

"Clarence," Edward admonished, but the older man was not put back and only waited for Kate to respond.

She laughed. "No. He wasn't taken to drink." She sliced the lemon squares in the opposite direction. "He was taken to womanizing. I caught him with someone, in our shared office no less, and called off our engagement on the spot. When he realized he couldn't—" She searched for an appropriate metaphor as she handed a lemon square to Clarence. "Have his cake and eat it, too, he went a little berserk, broke into my apartment, and destroyed everything in sight. Chuck had always been a thorough man. He was very thorough in the destruction of my things.

"Most of what I owned had belonged to my Grandma Katie. I couldn't bear the task of trying to replace it all. Thus" she waved her hand to show off her lack of decor—"I live as you see it."

Clarence took the square from her hand, then Kate produced a second square and handed it to Edward. He stood staring at her, seemingly lost in some thought for all of five seconds before he finally took the cake from her proffered hand.

"Your ex- . . . fiancé?" Edward finally asked.

Kate nodded. "Yes. You remember? I told you all about it over lunch—oh, some months ago."

Hesitantly, Edward nodded.

She continued for Clarence's benefit. "Well, except for a few obscene phone calls before I had my number changed and unlisted, I haven't heard from him in over five years."

Kate picked up the pan with the remaining lemon squares and carried them past Clarence and Edward to the living area. There, she was treated to Ned's praise for not having forgotten.

"And I'll even forgive you for planting me on the floor like this. Put another pan of lemony things in front of me and I won't even mind that I can't get up from the floor at the end of the evening."

Everyone except Ned stood now and stretched muscles un-accustomed to sitting on the floor.

"Harry's been complaining about sitting on the floor for the past half month."

"Yeah," Roland chimed in. "Seems I'm the only one hasn't had the pleasure yet. Where is he?"

Clarence answered. "With Claire, no doubt. They've been seeing a lot of each other lately."

Ned and Roland made teasing sounds. Kate looked sym-pathetically to Clarence, but he did not seem put off by the mention of Claire and Harry.

Kate leaned over to pick up Ned's empty glass from the table, then returned to the kitchen to refill it. She was just in the process of adding more ice when Clarence surprised her again by following her.

"Our friend, Tucker, seems pretty happy these days."

Kate turned, then smiled. "I hope so."

"I guess your promise came true."

"My promise?" Kate turned her full attention to Clarence, who spoke in an unmistakably secretive tone.

"You made your intentions clear early on." He nodded toward her ringed hand. "Seems everything is turning out as you planned.'' Clarence sounded neither congratulatory nor anxious.

Kate nodded, a half smile on her lips. "Then he *did* tell you. I'm glad.''

Laughter sounded from the next room and Clarence took a step further into the kitchen, offering their conversation greater privacy. "He talks about you nonstop. But he talks about Harry, too.'' Kate looked up at Clarence questioningly, so he continued. "His late wife—Ellen—she hurt him bad when she left him for another man. He makes his promises and goes into these commitments for life. He doesn't understand when other people break their promises. He was lost when Ellen left him and when she came back he tried to pretend she had never left him.

"He doesn't understand these modern romances and tries hard to justify your relationship.''

Kate was more confused than when she had begun talking with Clarence. She still felt as if Edward's friends were precisely that—*his* friends—and she was not comfortable asking Clarence to elaborate, but she thought she understood his kindly advice. Edward still felt an attachment to his late wife. That was why he had not made a move for Claire and how Harry had been able to beat him to the punch.

Kate took these disquieting thoughts with her as she and Clarence returned to the poker game, which lasted another two hours. Still, Edward made no announcement and Kate played awkwardly, trying not to make an obvious attempt at covering her engagement ring and yet feeling exposed each time the overhead light made the facets sparkle.

At last, her apartment door was closed behind the last of her guests. She did not consider Edward a guest and turned and smiled to see him quietly clearing the low table of glasses and napkins.

Kate fell to work beside him, tidying the poker things, depositing her near-empty cup of pennies into the corner behind her easel, and finally lifting the table to stand on its end and fit neatly in the closet. Edward closed the closet door, still without speaking, and it was Kate who finally broke the silence.

"You were very quiet all evening.''

He looked to her with a pleasing smile. "Hmm? Yes. You too."

"You told Clarence . . . about our engagement," she finished.

"Yes. He's known all along." Edward stopped folding the tablecloth to look over it at Kate, finally draping it over his arm.

"I only mention it because"—she swallowed, her courage for asking the question leaving her—"I thought you would tell your other friends."

"I hope they are your friends, too."

"Of course. I like them very much, but I didn't feel free to tell them." She laughed nervously. "I mean, their loyalties lie with you. Clarence is especially protective and I like him all the more for that. It's just that . . . I thought perhaps you were waiting to tell Claire first."

Edward finished folding the tablecloth, opening the closet again and depositing it on the top shelf before responding. "Have you told Harry?"

"No."

Edward took a step closer and gently lifted her left hand. He toyed with her ring. "Why not?"

Kate looked up at him, mesmerized by the flecks of brown in his mostly gray eyes. "To be perfectly honest, I haven't seen a lot of Harry over the past few days. He's been spending a lot of time with Claire."

"Ah," was his only response before dropping her hand and moving toward the kitchen.

Kate followed, only wanting him to take her hand again and eventually kiss her. He had not kissed her since the evening before his proposal. Usually, she thought, it was customary to kiss the woman to whom you were engaged.

Edward turned on the tap and began filling the sink with water, but Kate stopped him by putting her hand over his. "Don't. I can do this tomorrow morning. It's late."

"Oh, of course." And he looked down at the watch on his arm. "You're probably exhausted and I should leave you to get ready for bed."

He was already turning toward the door to the living area

when Kate stopped him again, this time with her hand on his forearm.

"I didn't mean to send you away. I want you to stay." With more nervousness than was outwardly visible, she stepped in front of him and slowly slipped her arms around his neck.

Edward displayed his nervousness as he tentatively put his hands on her waist.

Kate laughed, breaking some of the tension. "You can feel free to kiss me now."

Edward smiled, and bending his head, brushed her lips with his own. It was Kate who pulled him to her a second time and intensified their kiss. She held her breath as he relaxed and joined in the kiss, finally pulling away to look down into her eyes with seriousness.

"I think I would enjoy this more if I didn't have this fear that at any moment we were going to be joined by Harry."

Kate looked around his shoulder toward the front door, then tipping her head sideways, she inspected the watch on his wrist. "That's odd. Harry's usually back by now."

At that instant the phone rang, jarring Kate back to reality. She was suddenly swept by a premonition of doom. Why wasn't Harry home? She looked up at Edward with panic.

The phone rang again before Kate left Edward to snatch up the clunky black receiver from the floor.

"Hello?"

Edward took a step toward the phone as if he too knew something was amiss.

"Harry. Where are you?"

Kate was silent for a moment before she turned startled eyes to Edward. "Edward is here with me. The game has just broken up." There was a pregnant pause before Kate spoke again. "Yes, I know he'd want to hear it from you, too."

Kate passed the telephone to Edward, but could not bare to see his expression and turned away.

"Hello, Harry. Are you all right?"

Kate waited, holding her breath.

"You and Claire are *married?*"

Chapter Nine

Kate slapped her hand over her mouth as she leaned toward Edward to share the receiver and Harry's news.

"Now, I know we should have told you sooner, but we didn't want a lot of hubbub. We would have called right after the ceremony, but by then you'd be sitting down to poker and Claire wants to tell Clarence in person. Seems she thinks he might be a little upset that we ran off like we did." Harry snorted. "Like we was a couple of kids or something."

Claire could be heard in the background, her laughter like tinkling ice in a glass and Harry, turning to her, said, "Claire, honey, Edward's on the phone, too."

"Tucker?" Claire took the phone from Harry.

Kate looked at Edward's expression, her ear still close to his on the other side of the receiver.

"Claire, are you sure you know what you're doing?"

"Tucker. It *is* you. Now what are you two kids doing still together, and here it is nigh on . . . one in the morning!" she teased.

"Not the same thing you're up to."

Claire giggled like a schoolgirl. "Don't get fresh with me, Tucker." Then more seriously, she said, "Listen, Tucker. You have to keep my secret for me—at least until I get a chance to see Clarence. I tried to reach him earlier, but he had already left for Kate's house to play poker."

Kate thought to make her presence known. "I'm here, too, Claire."

"Well, it seems we're all just one big happy family now. How are you doing, Kate?"

Kate smiled. She could not be more thrilled with Harry's choice. Claire was everything she could have hoped for in a step-grandmother. The thought of the beautiful, classic Claire as her step-grandmother made her laugh aloud. "I'm in shock."

"Oh, dear." Claire turned to Harry. "She's in shock, but she's laughing, so I don't think she'll hold it against us for too awful long."

"So what are your plans?" Edward broke in.

"I'm not sure I know what you mean, Tucker. We were married at five P.M. today and tomorrow I think we're going to have tuna salad for lunch."

"I mean, where are you going to live? Are you running off on a honeymoon? Are you staying in the city or going to Harry's farm?"

"I don't know, Tucker. I've lived so long by schedules I think we're just going to be a little impulsive for a change."

Edward was stern. "Well, so far you've managed that. When can I see you?"

Again, Kate looked to the side of Edward's face.

"Oh, too many questions, Tucker. I'll catch up with you again—probably next week sometime."

"We'll call you later," Harry broke in, then to Kate he said, "You just take care, Katherine, and take care of that young man of yours."

Kate took over the receiver as Edward pulled away from the phone. "I will, Harry, and Harry? I love you."

She returned the receiver to its cradle.

Edward nervously paced his bedroom. How could he be expected to keep this from Clarence? Next to DaVinci, Clarence was his closest friend. Just a few months ago he might have turned to DaVinci for advice, but Kate would see right through any questions he might ask under the guise of Cyber Scribe.

Flipping the switch on the side of the computer, he waited for the screen to come to life while he walked to the bathroom to switch on his shower. It was closer to two in the morning. He had left Kate soon after the phone call from Harry and Claire and he could tell that she had been deeply disturbed by the news. She had put on a good show for Harry and Claire's benefit—pretending her stunned reaction was mingled with happiness for them, but Edward thought he had been able to see through the charade.

As soon as Kate had hung up the phone, he voiced his surprise. "I hadn't realized there was nothing standing in their way." Edward turned dumbly to Kate.

She sank to sit beside the telephone on the floor, but looked up at him. "They're in love, Edward. What's to prevent them?"

"I thought . . ." he stammered. ". . . paperwork, lawyers, whatever has to be done between getting a divorce and getting married."

Kate shrugged. "Divorce is a whole lot easier these days."

Edward nodded. "Then with Harry and Claire neatly settled there's nothing preventing us from setting a date."

Unable to bear the hurt in Kate's eyes as she looked up from the floor at him, he bent and kissed her. As he pulled away, a tear glistened on her cheek. He flicked it off with his thumb, then straightened.

"Will you have lunch with me tomorrow?"

Kate nodded, but did not speak. He touched the side of her cheek, then left.

Now he found himself wishing he had stayed with her. She was obviously devastated that Harry had been so successful in replacing her. She had made her feelings for Harry perfectly clear when she told him she still loved him. Edward had thought that Kate would want to be alone, but now he regretted his decision to leave her. He wanted to be able to comfort her.

Edward turned on the shower, then moved back out of the master bath toward his computer. There he logged on while still standing and unbuttoned his shirt with one hand.

"Cyber Scribe has entered the room."

He walked back to the bathroom to finish undressing. He only barely heard the ping as he was called back to his computer. He hastily turned off the faucet.

DaVinci: I was hoping you'd be on-line. I've missed our chats at a time when I've needed them most.

Cyber Scribe: I was just feeling the same way.

DaVinci: You first.

Cyber Scribe: Thanks. Do you remember my telling you about the married woman? The one who gave me a social kiss that I wished wasn't so social?

DaVinci: Vividly.

Cyber Scribe: Well, it seems she wasn't so married as I had believed.

DaVinci: And you missed out?

Cyber Scribe: Missed out?

DaVinci: Somebody else beat your time? You lost her to someone else?

Cyber Scribe: Not on your life! I wouldn't let that happen. There's the rub. She's in love with someone else.

DaVinci: How do you propose not to lose her then?

Cyber Scribe: That's what I'd like to ask you. How do I win her?

There was a long pause before Kate responded.

DaVinci: I'm not sure I'm the best person to ask.

Cyber Scribe: I'm certain you are the only person I could ask. What would make a woman fall out of love with one person and in love with another?

DaVinci: There are too many variables.

Cyber Scribe: Then imagine it was you. What qualities does the man possess who could win your heart?

DaVinci: Honesty.

Cyber Scribe: And?

DaVinci: That encompasses a lot. If he were honest with me—and with himself—he'd have my unfaltering devotion. That would entail being open. We would talk about everything under the sun. I wouldn't expect him to be perfect, but when I saw that he was making a mistake I'd feel free to tell him so.

Cyber Scribe: And vice versa?

DaVinci: Of course.

*Cyber Scribe: There's something I've been meaning to
tell you.*

*DaVinci: Don't. Please don't make any confessions—
least of all to me. I'm not sure I could take it tonight.*

*Cyber Scribe: I'm trying to win your "unfaltering de-
votion." You know, all that honesty stuff.*

*DaVinci: I lied. You already have my devotion. Just
please, no heart-wrenching confessions tonight.*

Cyber Scribe: Are you all right, friend?

DaVinci: Just a little low.

Cyber Scribe: Okay. It's your turn.

DaVinci: I too am a victim of unrequited love.

Cyber Scribe: Strangely parallel.

DaVinci: Yeah. Funny.

Cyber Scribe: You know you'll always have me.

DaVinci: I'm going to hold you to that.

Edward signed off, wishing Kate's sentiments mirrored
DaVinci's.

The next day, Kate, feeling the need for exercise, took the
stairs instead of the elevator up the four flights to Edward's
office. She recalled the first time she had come to his office
for the details of her illustrative assignment for the journal.
The science editor had been very inquisitive about her relationship with Edward. Kate suspected she had a crush on her
employer and was scoping out the competition. What, Kate
wondered, would the other woman think when she found out
Kate and Edward were engaged? What would anyone think if
they knew the nature of their one-sided relationship?

Kate reached the door at the fourth level and pushed it open.
The transition from concrete and metal railings to carpet and
soft music was blatant. The elevator doors beside the stairs
opened and an intern stepped out pushing a cart of mail. A
receptionist sat at the front desk looking immaculately coiffed.
On the wall behind her, large letters told those disembarking
from the elevator that they had just entered the offices of
Tucker Publishing.

Kate was about to move down the hall toward Edward's

office when the receptionist detained her. "Yes, ma'am. May I help you?"

Kate smiled, recalling herself. "Thank you, but I'm just going to meet Edward, er, Edward Tucker," she finished, remembering that the science editor had referred to him as Tucker and probably everyone who worked for him knew him by the same.

"And do you have an appointment, ma'am?" Kate had begun to pass the desk when the woman asked the question and held out a hand to detain her again.

"Ah, yes, I mean no, I mean . . ." Kate stammered.

The receptionist, still very polite, but very efficient in carrying out her duty of screening visitors, stood up. "If you'll just have a seat." She gestured toward a very comfortable chair in the reception area.

"Excuse me." Kate began to unravel her tongue. "I meant to say I don't have an appointment. I have a lunch date with Edward."

Again, the receptionist looked at her with skepticism, but hesitated in dialing the number that would connect her, supposedly, with her employer's office. Instead, the receptionist looked down at the watch on her wrist. Her action as much as told Kate that she did not believe her as it was still just a little past eleven—early morning by Kate's standards and far too early for lunch.

Finally, Kate gave the woman the evidence she wanted. Politely extending her hand, she announced, "I'm Kate, Edward's fiancée."

As soon as the words were out of her mouth, Kate regretted them. With the exception of Clarence, Edward had not told anyone at his office. By the end of the day the news would have spread like wildfire. If Edward had any notion of neatly backing out of their engagement, he could hang it up. Kate felt her stomach knot.

The receptionist hesitantly took Kate's proffered hand, then her face lit up. "Fiancée? How wonderful. Congratulations. I didn't know."

Kate shook her head, suddenly feeling very shy. "No,

ma'am I believe we only met the one other time I've been in the office, about a month ago.''

Nodding energetically now, she said, ''Yes, yes. I remember you.'' She tried to recall. ''I can't remember what you were here about, but . . .''

''No. No reason you should. I'm sorry, but I didn't catch your name.''

The receptionist blushed prettily. ''Janet. Janet Smith.''

''Well, Janet Smith, it's very nice to make your acquaintance.'' Kate was cordial on the outside, but inwardly she only wanted to put distance between herself and her blunder of indiscretion. This time the receptionist was compliant in allowing Kate to pass unannounced.

''Nice meeting you, too,'' the woman called after Kate.

Kate looked over her shoulder as a man approached the receptionist's desk. Janet Smith lost no time in telling him of the secret new fiancée and Kate stumbled on the carpeting as the man looked up from his tête-à-tête with the receptionist, craning his neck to check out the mystery woman.

It was in this fashion—stumbling, her nerves a-jangle and off-kilter—that Kate entered the office suite of the president of Tucker Publishing.

''Well, I'm sorry if you don't approve, Tucker. We didn't think to consult with you.''

Kate froze in her steps as she looked through the connecting door into Edward's office to see him with Claire. Edward sat perched on the front edge of his desk, his hand on Claire's elbow as she stood, defiant, just a foot away from him.

''And you know darn well I didn't mean to imply that you needed my approval. It's just . . . you know so little about this man. You've known each other just two weeks and you up and marry him. You don't know what he is or you would never have carried on as you have!''

Claire meant to turn away from Edward, but catching her elbow, he tried to detain her. ''Claire, don't be mad at me.'' His voice was suddenly soft. ''I wouldn't be saying any of this if I didn't care enormously about you. I only want you to be happy.''

Kate quietly turned and left the office before Edward or

Claire could notice her standing in the outer office doorway. Lost in her thoughts, she could only hear Edward's words to Claire as they repeatedly rang in her ears. *"You don't know what he is . . . I care enormously for you."* Kate felt she needed to escape. She made her way toward the lobby, and seeing nothing between herself and the stairwell door she aimed for that mark.

"Slow down." Clarence caught her as she barreled into him as he emerged from the copy room beside the reception area. "Kate! How nice to see you." The older man, still steadying her with two hands on her shoulders kissed her cheek. "A deck of cards and some club soda and we could have a poker party. Claire has just come to take me out to lunch. I think Harry's meeting us there. Oh, but you've just come from Edward's office. Did you see them?"

Kate swallowed the lump in her throat and painted on a smile. "Yes. I've just come from there. They seemed to be busy though, so I decided to wait out here." She pointed toward the reception area.

"Oh, nonsense. Come on back." Taking her elbow, he escorted Kate back to Edward's office suite. "Look who I bumped into," Clarence announced as they rounded the corner into the outer office.

Claire's color seemed to be more heightened than usual, but Kate thought, if she had not witnessed the heated discussion just a moment before, she might not have noticed that anything was amiss. Clarence did not seem to notice.

Edward moved from his perch on the edge of his desk and came through the door into the outer office. There he was natural in collecting Kate in a warm embrace and kissing her cheek.

His smile seemed genuine. "You're here early. I'm glad. I was getting hungry."

Kate's smile did not quite reach her eyes. How, she wondered, would she make it through lunch with Edward?

"Let me just grab my coat and wallet." He released her and made his way back into his office.

"Kate." Claire moved toward her and took up where Edward left off, giving her a fond embrace and a peck on the cheek. Secretly, she whispered, "We're taking Clarence out to lower the boom. Wish me luck." And pulling away, she gave Kate a sly wink.

"He can't help but be thrilled, Claire. I know I am." Kate was able to smile sweetly at Claire and felt a little bit of her own tension melt away.

"So where are you taking me?" Clarence spoke up after returning from the file cabinet on the other side of the room.

"Mmm, it's a surprise. In fact, I think you'll find that lunch is full of surprises today." Again, Claire winked at Kate.

Kate sank into a leather chair across from Clarence's desk. At least, she thought, Edward's sentiments were one-sided. After all, he had only met Harry on a very few occasions. Perhaps once he got a chance to know Harry a little better he would approve of the match with Claire. Once he saw how happy Claire and Harry really were, maybe then Edward would feel less inclined toward breaking them up.

Edward returned from his office after switching off his computer and grabbing his winter coat from the rack behind his door. Kate looked up and realized, at the very least, she owed Edward the courtesy of having lunch with him in order to inform him of her blunder earlier with the receptionist. He had to be told that she had spilled the beans about their being engaged.

"Well, you two have fun," Edward called over his shoulder to Claire and Clarence. He held his hand out to Kate. She found her hand drawn like a magnet into his and it only felt natural to walk out of the office without releasing his hand. "So if you don't have any objection, I've made reservations for us for lunch."

"I don't have a preference. I'm not really used to eating so early."

He had eyes only for Kate as they walked past the receptionist and he pressed the button to the elevator. "Good. Then I'll assume you came early because you wanted to see me." His smile might ordinarily have melted her had she not just overheard his conversation with Claire.

The elevator made a ping and they stepped on with their hands still locked together. The elevator doors were not quite closed when Edward stunned Kate by tipping her chin up and kissing her full on the lips. Neither saw the starry-eyed receptionist as she smiled after them.

Kate staggered against him. "What . . . what was that for?" Her voice was a throaty whisper.

"For having lunch with me."

Kate moved away, still steadying herself with her hands on his coat lapels. "I have to tell you something."

He looked down, studying her face. She could not meet his gaze and only lowered her eyes again. She knew she had to tell him what she had just overheard. Their relationship, if indeed they were to go through with their wedding, could not be based on secrets. She had to let Edward know that she knew how he felt about Harry and that he was in love with Claire.

"I accidentally told the receptionist that we were engaged." she hedged.

"Accidentally? Why accidentally?"

"I . . . you . . . you haven't told anyone yet, so I thought maybe you still weren't sure you wanted to . . ." but she could not continue.

Edward was shaking his head. "What would give you an idea like that?" He laughed, then kissed the top of her head and put a comforting arm around her shoulder. "I haven't told anyone yet, because you haven't told Harry. I thought you might like to tell him first." He threw up his hands. "But here he goes and scoops our good news with his own."

"Do you really think it's good news? Harry and Claire having married?"

He tipped his head. "A mixed blessing, I think. Claire has just left me in no doubt as to her own happiness. I don't know Harry all that well, but if you're confident that he will be good to her, then I suppose I'll just have to put faith in that."

Kate held her breath. Could Edward possibly have made such a shift in so little time? Kate put her hand on Edward's arm. "Oh, he will be. Harry will be a wonderful husband to Claire. Just wait and see."

He smiled again. "Then with that sort of recommendation I'll believe it to be true, too."

They left the elevator when it reached the underground garage. In the confines of his car, Kate felt more at ease about asking him the difficult questions. She fastened her seat belt, then turned to face him as he turned the key in the ignition.

"You care very deeply for Claire, don't you?"

Looking over his shoulder to check for traffic before backing out he answered Kate without looking at her. "Both Claire and Clarence mean a lot to me. Clarence practically had to bottle-feed me when my wife left and his sister did almost as much. Mind you"—he glanced at Kate with a smile—"Clarence is no ball of fun to live with. He stayed with me for a short while right after Ellen left. I can fully understand why his sister moved out. Claire is very particular about her home and Clarence is, let us say, not exactly a fussbudget."

Kate tried to process what Edward said. "Claire is Clarence's sister?"

Edward only nodded and kept talking as he maneuvered the car through the low-ceilinged lanes of the parking garage. Luckily, Edward held up the conversation the entire drive to the restaurant while Kate listened distractedly.

Her mind raced to put the pieces together. If Claire and Clarence were brother and sister, then who was the married woman with whom Edward was in love? While relieved to learn that Edward was not pining over Claire and had only friendly concern for her well-being, it was disturbing to Kate to think that she had been missing an entire piece of the puzzle.

Kate barely noticed where they were until Edward stopped the car and handed over his keys to the valet at the door. Kate allowed herself to be dumbly led through the double doors into the luxury hotel where they would be dining. Craning her neck to look at the ornate ceiling in the lobby, she almost did not hear Edward when he spoke.

"I thought, if you like the food, we could hold the reception here."

Kate gave him her full attention. "Reception?"

"Reception. It falls between wedding and honeymoon?"

Kate felt her cheeks flush, then she looked around at the grand hotel again and nodded appreciatively.

Edward chuckled and tucked her hand in the crook of his arm. "I love when you do that."

"Do what?"

"Blush at the mention of a honeymoon."

Kate felt her cheeks grow warmer, but she smiled, fully enjoying this intimacy with Edward. "Well, it's not like I've ever had one before. I know the artist crowd is supposed to be pretty bohemian, but I've really led a fairly tame lifestyle. I'm afraid you'll find that I'm pretty inexperienced in such matters."

Their conversation had to cease as they reached the doors to the restaurant and the maitre d' immediately appeared and found no trouble in seating them although they were early for their reservation. The intimacy they had shared, however, was not to be renewed when they were seated. Edward became conspicuously reserved and Kate found that it was she who had to broach the subject of their impending wedding again.

"You mentioned we might set a date today."

"If you don't mind, Kate, could we wait just a week longer before setting the actual date? I have some business to tidy up first and then I'll know precisely what my schedule is like for the next year."

She had never imagined waiting so long before they were married, but she well understood why he wanted to wait out the week. He wanted to reveal himself as Cyber Scribe on their date. She supposed he thought he was putting a lot on the line if Kate had not known all along that he was Cyber Scribe. Kate sat back in her seat, relaxed for the first time since they had been seated.

"Oh." Edward fished through the breast pocket of his jacket. "I did mean to give you this, though." He pulled out a key which he handed to Kate.

Kate looked down at it puzzled. "The executive washroom?"

Edward smiled and Kate imagined him making these same expressions when they chatted via the Internet. She longed to be able to sit up late at night talking with him and having only to look in his direction to see those same expressions.

"My apartment, or rather *our* apartment."

Again, Kate felt herself blush.

"I thought you might like to make some personal changes in the place. As the mood strikes you, you could move any of your things upstairs that you like. The larger stuff I can move some weekend, although I can't think of much that you own in the way of bulk."

Kate felt all fluttery inside. It was real. She had not thought about the logistics of being married to Edward. Somehow, though, rather than make her feel pressured as one might have expected, Edward's suggestions made her feel at once secure. At least he was thinking about their marriage in real terms.

"Thank you." She wrapped her hand around the key. "I'll do that—probably today if it's all right with you."

Just then, a waiter came to welcome them and to take their drink orders. Kate felt closer to Edward than she ever had as they enjoyed a meal together and chatted about the sort of commonplace things a longtime married couple might.

Edward paced from his office to Clarence's. The older man having taken off the remainder of the day, Edward felt alone with his thoughts. That was for the best, he thought. He usually liked to bounce ideas off of Clarence, but there were some thoughts that were just too private even to share with Clarence.

For example, what had Kate meant, in saying that she was pretty inexperienced in such matters? Honeymoons, or something else? Had she and Harry had a platonic relationship?

Edward shrugged and muttered to himself. "I'll just ask her."

As if the matter were settled he sat down at his desk, but he did very little work for the remainder of the day.

Edward came home to what now really felt like a home. As he turned his key in the door, he knew Kate would be hard at work in her new studio. There was a faint scent of turpentine from Kate's painting, but it was not unpleasant. It was mingled with the scent of fresh-baked bread. Music from a bluegrass band played on the stereo in the living room. Kate came out of the kitchen singing along.

" 'Lack a fox, lack a fox, lack a fox on the ru-un.' " She perfectly intoned the Southern twang and broke into giggles when she saw Edward standing in the middle of the living room with his hand on his hip, grinning at her. She quickly moved to turn down the stereo. "You could warn a person before you sneak up on them like that."

"What? And miss that performance?"

Kate was still laughing at herself. "Is this early for you to be home?" She glanced at the watch on her wrist.

"I missed you." He took two great strides and swept her up with an arm about her waist and kissed her. He was becoming accustomed to impulsive gestures toward Kate and she did not seem to mind. This was a side of himself he had never been free to express before.

Kate looked up at him smiling, still held to his side. "I missed you, too. You work a lot."

Edward nodded, but felt deceptive. Not more than thirty minutes ago they had been chatting with each other as Da-Vinci and Cyber Scribe and Edward had only wanted to be near her.

Suddenly, Kate pulled away and took his hand. "Hey, I've got something to show you." She started toward her studio and, still holding her hand, Edward followed. "Wait here," she instructed him outside the studio door, but he watched as she hurried inside and hastily covered the work on her easel with a canvas. "Okay. You can come in now." But as if she had not been hiding the work on her easel, she redirected Edward's attention by pointing toward the desk Harry had given her. Edward looked at her, feeling somewhat deflated by her actions. He did not want Kate to feel the need to hide anything from him. Instead of bringing attention to her furtive behavior, however, he only walked around to the side of the desk which Kate indicated.

Edward swallowed hard. Kate had managed to move her entire computer system upstairs by herself. While he had been chatting with her over the Internet today, she must have already had her computer set up in the studio. It nervously reminded him that everyday he was one day closer to having to reveal himself to Kate as Cyber Scribe. He had never thought of himself as a defeatist, but all along he had been telling himself it was all too good to last. Kate would find out who he was. She would feel completely betrayed and violated and she would never want to see him again. He felt his only hope was in having her so soundly situated in his apartment that she would at least have to give him a hearing before walking out on him.

Edward looked around the studio. The computer was not the only thing she had moved. The room was almost beginning to feel cozy. True, the floor remained largely uncluttered, but now a chair had been added. It had been painted black and the seat bore a homey, earth tone needlepoint cushion.

"When did you have time to do all this?"

Kate shrugged and looked around her at her handiwork. "I didn't do a whole lot of work today, that's for sure. I went out right after lunch to this little junk shop I know of and bought the chair. I had noticed it some time ago, but never thought I would have a use for it. I brought it home in a cab and the rest of the stuff is from my place. Bet you didn't think I had so much junk."

He smiled and shook his head.

"Then I was on the computer most of the afternoon. I only had time to move my artwork up here, then clean out a couple of brushes before I remembered I had left dough to rise in the kitchen and I had to stop to put it in the oven."

Edward's gaze returned to the computer. The new second telephone line was stretched across the studio from the jack on the wall. A screen saver had popped up, but he thought he would have liked to have seen which application Kate had been using. Was she still logged on to the chat group?

At that moment another thought occurred to him. Why hadn't Kate mentioned her impending date with Cyber Scribe? Was she keeping a secret from him greater than the canvas or her easel?

"So, what do you do on the computer?"

Kate distractedly switched off the monitor without switching off the CPU. "Oh, this and that. I mostly eavesdrop on other people's on-line conversations."

Edward felt a flare of jealousy, then thought how silly it was of him to be jealous of himself.

"You don't mind, do you?"

"Huh?" Edward was startled. Had Kate read his mind? "Mind what?"

Kate was scowling. "Mind that I've brought all this stuff up here. Maybe you're feeling a little bit invaded."

"Nonsense." He shook his head as well as breathed a sigh of relief for Kate's psychic inabilities. "I, ah," he stammered, "I'm just hungry. Trying to think of what to fix for supper."

Kate nodded, seemingly satisfied that he was telling the truth. They both turned and left the studio together, but in another furtive move, Kate pulled the door closed behind her. Edward followed her back toward the living room, but could not help but spare a curious glance over his shoulder toward the closed studio door.

DaVinci: So we're still on for tomorrow night?

Cyber Scribe: I'm going through with it.

DaVinci: You needn't make it sound like a trip to the guillotine.

Cyber Scribe: Don't you feel some trepidation?

DaVinci: That sounds pretty bleak.

Cyber Scribe: Nothing personal. Oh, it's just me. I'm going through some pretty huge life changes just now. I'm just waiting for it all to backfire and blow up in my face.

DaVinci: Tell me, just what is going on at home?

Cyber Scribe: Nothing much. Just the woman I love is planning a not-so-secret rendezvous with another man.

Kate suddenly sobered and pushed back in her new chair. The chair had an obnoxious squeak and it rolled noisily on the wooden floor. She would have to remember to get a small rug to go under it before it damaged the beautifully varnished floors.

DaVinci: Is this the married woman who turned out to be not so married as you had once supposed?

Cyber Scribe: One and the same.
DaVinci: I think I want to know more about this wo-
man . . .

It was difficult to believe that Claire was cheating on Harry.

. . . Have you known each other for long?
Cyber Scribe: Yes and no. We've known each other for
quite some time through the Internet, but we've only
been on a real-name basis for about four months
now . . .

Kate's heart began to pound.

. . . She's pretty indescribable. I can only say, she's
content to be with me, but I think her affections lie
elsewhere.
DaVinci: Perhaps you could tell me about her once we
meet in person?
Cyber Scribe: I'll tell you about her now. She thinks I'm
a kook.

Kate's heart skipped a beat. She scrolled to the top of the
screen to reread their conversation. *"Four months . . . married*
woman who turned out to be not so married." She recalled,
". . . a social kiss he wished was not so social." He was talking about her!

DaVinci: What makes you think her affections lie
elsewhere?
Cyber Scribe: She is still in love with her ex.

My 'ex.' Where the heck did you get that . . .'' Kate leaned
over the keyboard as if every stroke meant the difference between losing Edward forever or keeping him.

DaVinci: You seemed to think she had a pretty self-
destructive bent. You don't think her ex-husband was
good for her?

*Cyber Scribe: Heck no. The guy's an opportunist. I be-
lieve he took her in at a time when she was vulnerable.
And now that she seems to be really in love with him,
he's gone off and married another woman.*

Kate racked her brain to piece together Edward's misunderstanding about her.

*DaVinci: So you've met her ex-husband before?
Cyber Scribe: On several occasions. I've been able to
see firsthand that he's just all wrong for her. They have
little in common.
DaVinci: So, other than this lack of common interest, is
this fellow unlikable?
Cyber Scribe: No, which makes my dilemma all the more
annoying. Harry is a very likable fellow . . .*

"Harry?!" Kate literally jumped out of her chair sending it
crashing to the floor on its back. She hastily grabbed it up, all
the while watching the wall between the studio and Edward's
bedroom. Surely he must have heard that and he would wonder what she was doing. He did not seem to catch his own
slip-up, however, as he continued.

*. . . We've been thrown together in social situations
before. As charming as he may seem, I can't see the
attraction between them.
DaVinci: So why did you think they were married and
then come to realize they were not so married?
Cyber Scribe: I was told by someone that I should reconsider becoming involved with her because she was
married to someone else—that they were going
through a rough patch in their relationship and that
my interference might be the breaking point. I thought
they were only separated, but I found out they were
not so married as I had originally believed when this
man up and marries another woman on what seemed
an impulse. There was no paperwork nor lawyer.*

Kate snapped her fingers. That's what he had meant. It was not Claire and Clarence who had divorced. He was thinking of Harry and herself. But who, she wondered, could have told him that she was married—to Harry, of all people?

DaVinci: You know, friend, I think your prospects with this woman may be looking up soon.

Kate tried to suppress a laugh.

Cyber Scribe: I wish I had your optimism. Very soon I plan on laying it all on the line.
DaVinci: You're going to tell her how you feel about her?
Cyber Scribe: I'm going to tell her everything!
DaVinci: That's it. You just come clean and she's bound to respect you for that.
Cyber Scribe: Ugh! Respect. That's a poor substitute.

Kate hugged her middle as she signed off. She felt she might burst, but she would wait. She would make Edward stew just one night longer before she too came clean. She signed off, then quietly left her studio. Making as little noise as possible, she walked to Edward's bedroom door and turned the knob.

He was still seated at his desk. His hair was damp from having showered earlier in the evening and he wore sweat-pants under a navy flannel robe.

"I'm heading out now."

Edward jumped, then hastily pulled the rolltop down on his desk.

"You scared me to death," he explained.

"I'm sorry." She smiled sweetly, not in the least bit sorry, but taking secret delight in his discomfort. "I should have knocked first."

"No. This is your room, too."

Kate looked around the room and smiled. "I like it. My room at Harry's place was hideous. Purple and lavender. Yuck."

Edward scowled. "Lavender? Harry doesn't strike me as the lavender sort."

"Oh, a lot of things about Harry would surprise you."

Edward rose from his seat and moved toward Kate. She waited for his kiss and when it came, she lavished in the full splendor of his love for her. She felt she needed to keep pinching herself to make sure she was not dreaming, but she settled for clinging to the front of his robe and feeling the soft, cottony texture under her hands.

"Hmm, that was nice," he whispered gruffly and ran his hand down the back of her hair.

"Very."

With every ounce of willpower she possessed, Kate pulled away from Edward. "Almost too nice." She smiled impishly up at him. It was with as much effort that she left his apartment. The next time, she knew she would not leave him alone.

Kate sat in the sun-filled sitting room with a dainty porcelain cup between her thumb and fingers. When she noticed the remains of some oil paint in the tiny wrinkles on the back of one of her hands, she wished she had taken greater pains with her appearance this morning.

As it was, however, she had risen at the awful hour of 6:00 A.M. in order to meet Harry and Claire at Claire's apartment before they went out for the day. Kate had been none too surprised to arrive and find that not only had they not left the house yet, they had not risen from bed and it was nearing 8:00 in the morning.

For the few minutes it took them to pull themselves together, Kate had had the opportunity to be alone with her thoughts. She had all but pieced the riddle together. Somehow, and this was the only missing piece of the puzzle, someone had told Edward that she and Harry were married. Her story about her ex-fiancé had fed the flames of that misunderstanding and now she recalled with a laugh the few instances Edward had been concerned about Harry's violent temper. He had thought it was Harry who had vandalized her former apartment. Edward had been telling Kate of his love for her for months, only she had thought that he was talking about Claire.

After a brief and confusing explanation of the events of the past few months, Claire got on the phone to her brother.

"Well, leave his coffee to drip a while longer, Clarence. It can wait. Listen to what I'm saying. Kate is here with Harry and me and she can confirm that wild story you were telling me yesterday." There was a short pause on Claire's end while Clarence, already at the office, filled his sister's ear. "No. Of course not. She's his granddaughter. We don't know how Tucker got this cockamamie story." Claire giggled before continuing. "Probably the same place Kate got the silly notion that I was married to you and that I was the married woman Tucker was in love with."

"Well, let me tell you, it clears up a whole lot," Harry muttered from the other side of the small serving tray where he sat across from Kate.

Kate looked around the room. Lace and roses were the theme throughout Claire's house. She could only imagine what Claire would think once she saw Harry's house. It was done in a very barren, Shaker style, if one could attribute any style to the home where Kate had lived with her grandfather. Harry seemed to be completely at home, however, holding his own Moss Rose coffee cup and serving himself sugar cubes with the dainty sterling silver tongs.

"Well, just do her a favor, will you? Don't let on to Tucker that you know anything more about Kate and Harry. Let Kate have that pleasure tonight when she has dinner with Tucker."

There was a short pause before Claire turned to Kate. "Clarence says Tucker already has something penciled in on his calendar for this evening—something he's been planning for months now."

Kate nodded, setting her cup down on its saucer. "Yeah. It's me—only I'm not supposed to know it's me."

"What?" Claire shook her head, then turned back to the phone. "She knows all about it, Clarence. She says it's her."

Kate added, "Only don't let him know that I know it's a date with me."

Claire shook her head. "Just don't say anything. It's too confusing to repeat."

As she closed her phone call to Clarence, Claire was laughing. "Oh, to be a fly on the wall tonight on your date."

"Please, Claire." Kate looked worried. "Please don't let on to anyone else. Edward would be mortified. I can't think if he's going to be angry with me as it is. After all, I've been keeping as many secrets from him. For months now, I've known that the man I fell in love with over the Internet was Edward."

Claire took the seat next to Harry. She served herself coffee without looking. Instead, she stared wide-eyed at Kate. "You found out that night—that night of the poker game, didn't you?"

Kate nodded, then turned to her grandfather apologetically.

"Say you forgive me, Harry, for not telling you before?"

Harry shook his head. "I can well imagine why you didn't. I'm not sure I understand it all now. I'd have been less confused if you had just kept it all to yourself."

This was not the overly protective grandfather Kate had known two weeks ago. This was a man in love with a wife and concerns of his own. She was glad for him.

"Well, if you'll both excuse me, then," Kate rose to leave. "I have a lot of preparing to do before tonight."

Harry kept his seat, but Claire rose again and gave Kate a motherly peck on the cheek. "I couldn't be more pleased for you, Kate. Next to Harry and Clarence, Tucker's about the most important man in my life. I couldn't be more happy for him and I know you'll make him happy."

"Just wish me luck tonight, Claire. I'll be happy if he's still speaking to me tomorrow."

Edward was taking off his overcoat as he entered the office suite. Clarence turned abruptly from the coffee maker on the credenza.

"Morning."

"Good morning, Tucker." Clarence wore a grin like a possum.

Edward moved toward his office, then turned back, throwing his coat over his arm. "What's gotten into you?"

Clarence just shook his head. "Oh, I don't know. Spring fever or something."

Moving toward his office, Edward paused and looked over his shoulder two more times, then disappeared behind his office door wondering what had gotten into the grinning secretary.

Since waking that morning Edward had been running late. As it was, it was nearly 9:30 before he sat down with his cup of coffee and flipped on his computer, having no idea that Kate—DaVinci—would be on-line.

He was dreading the entire day, because as the minutes ticked by he was closer and closer to the moment when Kate would undoubtedly disavow herself of him. It was with no little bit of surprise that he logged on then and popped into the middle of a conversation between DaVinci and Bronte.

"Cyber Scribe has entered the room."

Bronte: My knowledge of the publishing industry is limited. I'm a writer, so I'm lurking to try and get a glimmer of how the whole process works—maybe get an inside tip on some of the markets.
DaVinci: That was initially my reason for lurking on this chat group, too.
DaVinci: Good morning, Cyber Scribe.
Cyber Scribe: Good morning, DaVinci. You're up bright and early this morning.
DaVinci: Oh, I'm a real morning person. Up every day at the crack of dawn. To bed by sundown.

Edward scowled at his monitor.

Brontë: Well, it was nice chatting with you, DaVinci. I'd better get to work here. If my boss sees me whittling away the hours, I'll be done for. My writing doesn't make me any money, so I've got to keep this temp job to keep a roof over my head.
DaVinci: I'm in complete sympathy with you there. If I didn't work at this fast-food joint down the street I'd

be living out on it. Good luck with your writing and
keep at it.

Edward pushed away from his keyboard and squinted as if
he were reading DaVinci's message incorrectly.

DaVinci: Now, Cyber Scribe, are we still on for tonight?
You haven't chickened out yet, have you?
Cyber Scribe: Not on your life. But hey, what did you
mean about working at the fast-food joint down the
street—and what's this about keeping bakers' hours?
I thought you made a living as an artist and that you
kept really erratic hours.
DaVinci: I wish. That sounds like my dream life—but no.
I have to be up at the crack of dawn with all the other
stiffs in the world and get out and earn a living flipping
burgers.
Cyber Scribe: I'm confused. How do you write to me all
hours of the day and night and work at what must be
an incredibly labor-intensive job?

There was a long pause before DaVinci could answer.

DaVinci: Sorry there, Scribe. I had to lift the fries out of
the deep fryer. Oh, I manage.
Cyber Scribe: Oh, I get it. You're joking.
DaVinci: Keeping a roof over my head is no joke. What?
You trying to back out of our date now that you know
I work at a fast-food joint?
Cyber Scribe: No way. I'll play along.

Just then, Clarence popped his head around Edward's office
door.

"Phone for you, Tucker."

Edward grabbed the receiver and distractedly tucked it between his ear and shoulder. "Tucker here."

"Hello, Edward."

The receiver fell to his desktop with a crash at the sound

of Kate's voice. Hastily, Edward snatched up the receiver again. "Kate? Is that you?"

"Well, of course it is. What other sleepy-sounding female did you expect to be calling you at the office at this hour of the morning?"

Edward looked to his watch, then to his monitor.

DaVinci: You'd just better. I don't want to find myself stood up at the Flaming Flamingo tonight.

"Oh no."

"Edward? Are you okay?"

"What?" He was terse, then he softened. "Oh, Kate. Kate, I've made a horrible fool of myself. I think I've made a disastrous mistake."

"A mistake? What are you talking about?"

"Tonight, Kate, I've—"

"Oh yes, about tonight. You told me one time that your favorite food was lasagna. How about I whip you up a vat of my lasagna à la Katherine?"

"Tonight? No. Tonight I've made plans."

"Oh? No matter. I can make lasagna for you another time."

"No! I mean . . ." Edward ran a sweaty hand through his hair. "Yes. Tonight is fine. I've got to cancel the plans I had made."

"Don't do that, Edward. I mean, lasagna can wait. I realize that you have a busy schedule. I lose sight of that because I set my own hours. I guess I'm pretty spoiled in that way."

"No, Kate. I'm definitely canceling. I've made a horrible mistake."

"Edward? Is something wrong?"

"I—I can't tell you over the phone. I'll have to see you in person."

"You sound upset. Do you want me to meet you for lunch?"

"I'm coming home. Can you meet me upstairs in, oh, say thirty minutes?" He looked back to his monitor.

DaVinci: Giving me the silent treatment now?

"Oh, for Pete's sake!"

"Edward. What's wrong?"

"Thirty minutes, Kate. My feet are hitting the floor running."

"Be careful and Edward?"

Leaning forward, he was preparing to hang up. "Yes?"

"I love you."

"I love you, Kate. Please remember that."

❦

It was Kate who hit the floor running. With Edward's living room telephone extension in her hand, she began wrapping the hundred feet of extra phone line around her hand and elbow as she walked back to the living room of the terrace apartment. There, she unattached the long cord and reattached the shorter wire.

She dashed back down the hall to the studio where her computer cursor blinked.

DaVinci: Giving me the silent treatment now?

Hers was the last message on the chat group. True to his word, Edward had not even bothered to respond and must have dashed out of his office to head home. Kate wondered, if the charade had a longer life span how would Edward, rather, Cyber Scribe, break things off with DaVinci. She almost felt sorry for DaVinci. It almost felt like a friendship was ending. She reminded herself that that particular friendship was actually evolving.

Putting herself into gear, Kate, unlike Edward, took the time to log off before walking to the easel in the middle of the studio floor. There, the canvas was still wet. Always her own worse critic, Kate would have liked to let the painting sit on her easel another month while she fine-tuned the housewarming gift she had begun for Edward months ago.

Dipping her paintbrush into the tin of turpentine, she used the solvent to blend two colors just a bit more. She stood back to examine what would have to be the final product. In the painting, a very realistic representation of a computer monitor held center stage while the coiled cord from the keyboard carried the viewer's eye across the canvas. The reflection of Kate's face looked out from the monitor while the back of what was unmistakably Edward's head weighted one side and lower corner of the painting. The foreground and background were littered with the objects that represented their special moments together—an elevator control panel, a small framed picture of Harry, and some playing cards scattered in the foreground. Edward's left hand rested on a keyboard while his right touched the screen. Immediately under the finger touching the screen, the monitor rippled like disturbed water. It was this rippling which Kate blended with her paintbrush.

It had been her intent to give the painting to Edward tonight at the restaurant, but that had seemed too public a place for sharing something so secret, so intimate. Kate worked another fifteen minutes, then gently lifted the meter-wide canvas and carried it to the living room.

No sooner had she turned after placing the canvas over the mantel above the gas fire than she heard Edward's key turn in the door. He had not wasted time and had arrived home ten minutes under his estimated thirty. Kate waited with a smile of greeting on her lips as he opened the door.

"Darn!" Edward grabbed his car keys from his top desk drawer and moved around his desk in one even stride. Clarence was just returning to his office and he and Edward collided as they both rounded the corner at the same time.

Edward caught Clarence by both arms and steadied him, then without explanation, kept moving down the hall.

"Now where you off in such a hurry?"

Edward turned, walking backward. "Home. I've really screwed up, Clarence. I've made a horrible mistake and it's gotta be fixed. I have to tell Kate everything. She's going to hate me."

"Whoa there." Clarence jogged after him, finally laying a hand on Edward's arm at the lobby elevator. "Why do you think she's gonna hate you? The woman loves you."

"No. Don't you see? She's still in love with Harry. He's in love with Claire and I fell in love with some woman I don't even know."

Clarence laughed loudly, attracting the attention of the receptionist who, Edward was sure, had been eavesdropping anyway.

"The two of you are the most ridiculous match there ever was. Now what's this about falling in love with someone you don't know?"

Edward took a deep breath. At the same instant, the elevator doors opened, so taking Clarence by the arm, he pulled him onto the elevator with him. At least their conversation would have some privacy until they reached the garage in the basement.

"It's like this. I met this woman over the Internet. For over a year we've been conversing and sharing—everything. I was attracted to this woman. I wanted to get to know her better, so I did a search and it turned out that this woman was Kate—or so I thought! Because I thought it was Kate I made a point of getting to know her better. I fell in love with her, but lo and behold, I find out she's married—to Harry of all people. Later, it turns out, they must have been divorced and I only thought they were still married, because Harry goes off and marries your sister, but I know Kate's still in love with Harry—heaven only knows why."

The elevator pinged and Edward, after glancing at the lighted panel to see they had arrived at the basement, began backing off of the elevator while still trying to fill Clarence in on the rest of his tale before being separated by the sliding doors.

"That's okay, though, because I love Kate and I believe she at least cares strongly for me, then two seconds ago I discover that the woman I met through the Internet and with whom I have a date for tonight isn't Kate at all, but some woman I don't even know."

To Edward's surprise, Clarence followed him out of the elevator and opened the passenger side door of his car to climb in.

"What are you doing?"

Clarence, wearing an enormous grin, merely slipped into the passenger seat. "Oh, this is too sweet to miss."

"Clarence, I'm not taking you with me when I go to break up with the only woman in the world I love."

"Now, just hold your horses. Nobody's breaking up with nobody. You're both a couple of numbskulls and you deserve each other."

Edward just shook his head.

"You know, Tucker, there's a male bonding thing that just goes beyond promises to a third party."

"What are you talking about?" Edward finally sat down behind the wheel of his car.

"Just that I think there's been enough confusion about who loves who and who's married to who and who's *going* to marry who." Clarence fastened his seat belt. "You drive and I'm gonna fill you in on a few facts you've been missing out on."

Hesitantly, Edward fastened his own seat belt, then paused to glance at his old friend before finally turning the key in the ignition.

Kate wrung her hands, but as nervous as she was, she could not erase the smile from her lips. She heard the jangle of keys, then saw the doorknob turn, then more slowly, the front door open.

Unlike herself, Edward was not smiling. He was the picture of severity. Kate immediately regretted leading him to believe that she and DaVinci were two different people. She ran to him and threw her arms around his neck. Pulling his head down she kissed him and would have continued the kiss had he not pulled away from her.

Taking her arms in his hands, he held her at a distance, looking down at her as if his world were about to end.

It was Kate who spoke first. "Please don't look at me like that."

His expression softened, but it was sad.

"Kate, I've done something so stupid." He shook his head. "I thought you might hate me when I told you tonight, but I'd much rather face that scene tonight with you than the one we're about to have."

"You thought I'd be upset?" She ran her fingers through

the graying hair at his temple. "Just wait until you hear what *I* have to tell you."

"No, Kate. Wait." He released her arms, then turned away from her. He turned back, about to speak, then stepped past her.

Kate held her breath. He paced into the sitting area of the living room and stopped right in front of the gas log fire. It seemed to Kate as if he looked straight through the painting, yet he never noticed it. He turned back around toward her, the same grim expression on his face.

"I've fallen in love with someone I met through the Internet. I can't explain how it happened. We have little in common and heaven knows I never meant to hurt you, but this can't be ignored."

Kate immediately sobered. She was jealous—of herself? "Edward, there's something I have to tell you."

"No. Wait. Let me finish. I can't put these feelings aside and we would never be happy together since she lives in this building. It would always haunt us."

"Edward, I . . ."

Edward stepped forward, taking both of Kate's hands in his. "It's no use, Kate. I love her." He stroked the back of her hand. "And you will love her too when you get to know her. You've already met her."

Confused, Kate could only shake her head.

"You found me out long ago. You caught me taking groceries to her door one night. It's Mrs. Gaines, the Vanilla Lady."

Kate took a step back. "Vanilla Lady!"

Edward was smiling now and took a step forward, taking her hands again. "Yes, Kate. Vanilla Lady. She is the only woman for me. She is my soul mate, my cyborg love, my destiny."

"Your destiny!" She shook her hands free and took another step backward. "It's not Vanilla Lady. It's me!"

"Careful, Kate." Again, he stepped forward and took her hands. "You're about to bump my new painting and I think it's still wet."

"Careful, my eye." She stopped suddenly, looking up at

Edward, who was looking down at her with laughter in his eyes.

He whispered, "That was a horrible trick to play on me." At the same time, he pulled her against his chest, allowing one hand to hold her at the back of her neck. "You deserved to be punished."

As realization that the hoax was up dawned on Kate, her stomach made a giddy lurch and she encircled Edward's middle with a bear hug.

"That is about the meanest thing anyone has ever done to me." She kissed him hard on the lips just to prove her point.

"Was it any meaner than telling me you were a short-order cook who lived in a cardboard box on the street?"

"And Vanilla Lady, of all people," she continued, ignoring his gibe.

"But I *love* Vanilla Lady." Softly kissing the underside of her wrist, he inhaled the scent of the vanilla extract which Kate had made a habit of wearing. Her hand caressed his cheek and he pressed his lips to hers, kissing her with an intensity that made her knees feel weak.

"And I love Cyber Scribe. I can't tell you what a dilemma that was causing me—trying to decide between my best friend or the handsome, unapproachable man upstairs."

"And did you know that I was eating my heart out over Harry?"

Kate nodded sadly. "I didn't know until last night."

Edward cocked his head. "Last night?"

"Yes. Your cover slipped. I mean, I knew you were Cyber Scribe. I've known for months—since the first time I came here to meet your friends over a game of poker. I put away their coats in your room and saw the screen saver on your computer and the chat group on-line. I didn't know, however, that the 'married woman' you were in love with was me. I never suspected that you thought Harry and I were . . ." But she trailed off. The entire notion was just too ridiculous. "Where on earth did you ever get such a silly idea?"

Edward looked backwards over his shoulder, saw the new sofa, aimed for it, then pulled Kate back into the chair with him. "That no-account agent of yours, of course."

Kate slapped her forehead. "David Tipton. Of course." But she was not terribly angry with him. David Tipton had all but told her the night he came to her apartment. She would not expect her agent to be eaten up with guilt over something he would deem trivial. Kate smiled. "That sounds typical of David. Only he would be brazen enough to concoct something as ludicrous as that and expect it to be believed."

"You like him, don't you?"

Kate smiled up at Edward. She was seated beside him with her legs casually across his lap, one arm behind his neck, the other hand on his shirtfront. "I like him. He's a scoundrel and rude and egocentric and extremely good at what he does."

"Well, I suppose I could learn to forgive him."

Kate kissed Edward's cheek again.

"So, DaVinci." Edward's gaze shifted to the artwork over the mantel. "You've been pretty busy."

Kate looked to the painting and smiled. "It was going to be a housewarming gift for completing your renovations, but how about a wedding gift?"

Edward nodded, then rose and moved across the room to gain a closer look at the painting. There, he shook his head and placed a hand on either side of the painting. "If only I had known, I might have been spared so much grief over Harry."

"And if only I had known that you thought I was married to Harry I might have been spared so much grief over Claire." She stood and moved to stand beside him.

Edward laughed. "Yeah. Clarence told me in the car on the way over."

"He told you! But he promised."

"Clarence said there was a bond of friendship that just went beyond promises to third parties."

Standing on her tiptoes, Kate linked her fingers behind Edward's neck. "I'm going to miss my Internet chats with my best friend."

"Then don't stop. I'm not going to give up my relationship with DaVinci."

"Keeping time with another woman? Then I'm going to keep company with my Internet friend."

"I hope so, but let's not be separated by four floors and a computer screen."

With that, he kissed her, pulling her so close she felt as if she might be a part of him—and on another level, she knew she was. They would never be separated by four floors again.

DaVinci: I'm not quite sure how to break this to you, friend, so I'll just out with it. I was married today.
Cyber Scribe: What a coincidence. Me too!
DaVinci: Anyone I know?
Cyber Scribe: Someone from my building. I think you'd like her if you ever met.
DaVinci: When will I ever get to meet you?
Cyber Scribe: There's no time like the present.

Kate signed off, but before she had rounded the corner from her studio, she collided with Edward. He had freshly showered and his hair still glistened with water droplets.

"You look just like I thought you would."

His hands moved to her waist and he pulled her close until she could feel his warmth through his robe.

"And you feel just like I thought you would." He led her into the new workspace that would be theirs after their wedding day. The shades were pulled, yet the room shimmered with the warm glow of light as the computer screen danced with a screen saver that read: *"Cyber Bride."*